"You Kn... These...

Dax asked Jillian, his expression strangely intense.

She looked at him sharply. "What?"

"Memories and someone to share them with."

Her eyes, wide and blue as a summer sky, were luminous as she nodded.

"I feel alone, too," Jillian said with an odd tone in her voice. Abruptly she turned away. "Let's just forget it, Dax."

He stepped closer, standing directly behind her without touching her. "I've discovered that I like remembering."

"I don't. It's better just to forget things." There was such sadness in her voice that he turned her to face him. Slowly he drew her to him. She didn't resist, and gently Dax pressed her head against his shoulder.

And for the first time since he'd set foot in town again, Dax felt as if he had truly come home....

Dear Reader,

Spring is in the air—and all thoughts turn toward love. With six provocative romances from Silhouette Desire, you too can enjoy a season of new beginnings...and happy endings!

Our March MAN OF THE MONTH is Lass Small's *The Best Husband in Texas*. This sexy rancher is determined to win over the beautiful widow he's loved for years! Next, Joan Elliott Pickart returns with a wonderful love story— *Just My Joe*. Watch sparks fly between handsome, wealthy Joe Dillon and the woman he loves.

Don't miss Beverly Barton's new miniseries, 3 BABIES FOR 3 BROTHERS, which begins with *His Secret Child*. The town golden boy is reunited with a former flame—and their child. Popular Anne Marie Winston offers the third title in her BUTLER COUNTY BRIDES series, as a sexy heroine forms a partnership with her lost love in *The Bride Means Business*. Then an expectant mom matches wits with a brooding rancher in Carol Grace's *Expecting....* And Virginia Dove debuts explosively with *The Bridal Promise*, when star-crossed lovers marry for convenience.

This spring, please write and tell us why you read Silhouette Desire books. As part of our 20th anniversary celebration in the year 2000, we'd like to publish some of this fan mail in the books—so drop us a line, tell us how long you've been reading Desire books and what you love about the series. And enjoy our March titles!

Regards,

Joan Marlow Golan
Senior Editor, Silhouette Desire

Please address questions and book requests to:
Silhouette Reader Service
U.S.: 3010 Walden Ave., P.O. Box 1325, Buffalo, NY 14269
Canadian: P.O. Box 609, Fort Erie, Ont. L2A 5X3

THE BRIDE MEANS BUSINESS
ANNE MARIE WINSTON

SILHOUETTE *Desire*®
Published by Silhouette Books
America's Publisher of Contemporary Romance

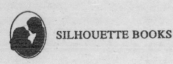 SILHOUETTE BOOKS

ISBN 0-373-76204-6

THE BRIDE MEANS BUSINESS

Copyright © 1999 by Anne Marie Rodgers

Books by Anne Marie Winston

Silhouette Desire

Best Kept Secrets #742
Island Baby #770
Chance at a Lifetime #809
Unlikely Eden #827
Carolina on My Mind #845
Substitute Wife #863
Find Her, Keep Her #881
Rancher's Wife #936
Rancher's Baby #1031
Seducing the Proper Miss Miller #1155
The Baby Consultant #1191
Dedicated to Deirdre #1197
The Bride Means Business #1204

* Butler County Brides

ANNE MARIE WINSTON

has believed in happy endings all her life. Having the
opportunity to share them with her readers gives her
great joy. Anne Marie enjoys figure skating and working
in the gardens of her south-central Pennsylvania home.

For Foxy
1979-1998

It still seems as if you just left me yesterday.
Purr in peace, my Old Girl.

One

A drop of sweat slipped between her shoulder blades, caught for a moment on the barrier of her bra, and then slithered on down the very middle of her back. As Jillian Kerr negotiated the uneven ground in her very high heels, her black summer suit felt as if it had turned to heavy wool. The sun was bright, and beneath her fingertips, the dark jacket of her escort felt hot.

After a week of rain, Baltimore had enjoyed three gorgeous days of nice weather, the wonderful Indian-summer weather for which mid-Atlantic Septembers were famous. The ground had dried, the grass was thick and green, summer birds still spread their song on the air.

Jillian didn't notice any of it.

The twin graves were a freshly slashed scar in the expanse of mown lawn as she walked around them to the canopy where the graveside service would be conducted. She released the arm of the friend at her side, and he dropped back to stand behind her with other friends from the stores near hers as she took a seat, alone, on the folding chairs reserved for family.

Only there was no family. Other than her, and she didn't really count. She and Charles had grown up together, were practically sister and brother, but in the most accurate sense of the word, they hadn't been related. And Alma, Charles's wife, was an only child of deceased parents, so there was no one there to represent her, either. Jillian was the only family there was left to mourn either of her two dear friends.

Well, that wasn't strictly true; there *was* other family. She had sent a very correct and courteous facsimile to share the sad news. But in her heart she was sure that she was the only one who would care enough to show up here today.

Carefully, she sidestepped the land mines in that train of thought and came out on the other side of sorrow as the minister began the service and the hushed voices in the crowd quieted. Her eyes stung, and she blinked once, shaking back her mane of blond hair and staring fixedly past the identical white caskets at the trees on the far side of the hill. She didn't cry. Ever. She repeated the words over and over as the clergyman eulogized Alma Bender Piersall and Charles Edward Piersall, local businessman, tireless community volunteer, active church member, generous contributor to many charities and her dearest childhood friend.

Charles Edward Piersall also had been responsible for the devastating sequence of events that had taken her only chance at love and made her who she was today. And still, even though she probably should have hated his sorry butt, her memories of Charles were warm and filled with love.

They'd ridden tricycles and bicycles together, played kick-ball and climbed trees. They'd gone skinny-dipping in the creek as teens until his father found out and tanned their fannies, criticized each other's dates and walked arm-in-arm to their high school graduation ceremony. They'd been there for each other during the darkest periods in each of their lives. And although she hadn't seen as much of him in recent years, the knowledge that Charles had been just across the city had been a sort of lifeline, an anchor when the loneliness threatened to overwhelm her.

A ripple of whispering in the crowd behind her caught her attention and she glanced around, annoyed at the commotion, preparing to quell the chatterers with one of her best freezing stares. Honestly, people today had no sense of propriety. Or plain good manners.

Movement caught her eye. It was—*it couldn't be!* As she recognized the dark head surging toward the front of the crowd, for one strange moment the ground rose up at her, tilted crazily, and settled back down only when she took a deep breath. She whipped her head back and faced front again, just as Charles's older brother Dax—Travers Daxon Piersall the *Fourth,* if you please—stepped from the crowd and walked to her side, folding himself into the chair on her right.

Oh, God. *He wasn't supposed to be here.* Panic rose. She nearly bolted from her chair before she remembered where she was, and she forced her quivering muscles to stillness. Flight was not an option. *Besides,* she told herself grimly, *you aren't the one who makes a habit of running away.* That thought brought forth such a surge of unexpected rage that she clenched her hands into fists, fighting the resentment and hurt that had hardened into pure hatred years ago. She'd be *damned* if she'd let Dax's unexpected, *unwanted* arrival chase her away.

The buzz of conversation grew fiercer, and in her peripheral vision, she saw his head turn. And the crowd grew quiet.

Why, oh, why hadn't he gotten flabby around the middle or worn bottle-thick glasses? Walked with a cane. Been follically challenged? *Any* little flaw would have done.

She hadn't taken more than that one horrible glance of identification, but it had been enough to show her that Dax hadn't lost one iota of his looks. If anything, his dark masculine presence had only intensified in his years away, and his shoulders looked as broad and strong as ever. The long thigh resting just to the right of her own, mere inches away, stretched taut over lean, muscled flesh hidden beneath the sober dark suit pants. A memory of that thigh, and the ecstasy it had brought pushing between her own, tried to roll across the mental screen in her head, and she ruthlessly chopped it into a million pieces.

Thank God she hadn't let her own figure go. Thank God. She looked damn good and she knew it. Her body was in great shape, courtesy of her never-ending calorie-counting, the stair machine, the free weights and legions of expensive skin lotions and hair appointments. Her nails were flawlessly lacquered in an appropriate, understated pale peach, her hair perfectly styled, and her black summer suit, bought during a terrific sale at a cute little boutique at Owings Mills Mall, fit every slender, sculpted, hard-earned curve perfectly.

Damn him. If only he'd wilted a little around the edges of his youth and good health. It would have been wonderful if she could have looked at him, this man she'd loved and had planned to marry, and wondered what she'd ever seen in him in the first place. Instead, she could barely breathe, and her heart was galloping away, leaving the rest of her to be dragged along behind by a stirrup.

The crowd behind her murmured, "Amen," and she realized they'd come to the conclusion of Charles's and Alma's funeral service. The minister stepped aside and she rose to do her part.

Beside her, Dax also stood. As she moved forward with two yellow roses, a last token of her friendship, he slipped his hand beneath her elbow, wrapping long fingers around her upper arm and holding her firmly against his side.

She cast him a furious glance, tugging her elbow away, but he didn't let her go. For the first time, their eyes met, and the cynical amusement she read in his black eyes made her grit her teeth so hard she heard them grinding together. If he thought he was going to force her into making a scene here, he was sadly mistaken. She'd come to pay her last respects to his younger brother—

Charles. Oh, God, Charles and Alma. The fight went out of her and she had to lock her knees against the sudden weakness that threatened.

The reason for Dax's presence exploded in her mind again. Charles couldn't be dead, couldn't be lying in cold abandoned silence in that white box. He was the only person in the whole world who knew everything there was to know about Jillian Elizabeth Kerr, and she needed him. She needed his undemanding friendship, the total support he'd always offered, the shoulder for her tears.

And Alma. Sweet, gentle Alma. Charles hadn't expected to love her, but she'd been the best thing that could have happened to him, and she'd accepted Jillian's place in his life as easily as she would have a real sister. Alma's shoulder also had been dampened by tears, though Jillian had stopped shedding them years ago.

But those tears were trying desperately to get out today. She pressed her lips together to still their quivering, standing silently for a moment before leaning forward to lay down her offering atop each casket, then moving aside so others could pay their respects.

Dax's fingers touching her arm burned through the suit cloth and as soon as she wasn't the focus of attention any more, she did yank her arm away. "Get your hands off me, Dax, unless you want to lose those fingers."

They had moved out into the sunlight, and his perfectly-cut black hair gleamed, so deep a midnight hue that not the slightest trace of copper or indigo highlight would dare show itself. He looked every inch the successful American male. He chuckled at her words, though there was no humor in the sound, and his deep voice raked over exposed nerve endings like sugar on a bad tooth. "I'm glad to see you're as charming as ever, honey-bunch. I just got into town. Aren't you going to fall all over me and welcome me home?"

"You're about seven years too late." She could have cut out her tongue as soon as the words came out—the last thing she wanted was for him to think his leaving had bothered her so much she still remembered it. But the old endearment had rattled her, brought memory nudging again at the door closed and locked on that chapter of her life.

His eyes narrowed, and something dark and scary moved beneath the polished charm for a moment, making her almost—*almost*—step back. But she wouldn't give him that satisfaction.

His eyes cut toward the coffins behind them. "Shame about old Charlie. And his wife. I never met her but she really must have been some hot number, for him to drop you like a hot potato."

Monster. How could he talk so callously about his own brother? The fist around her heart squeezed painfully, but all she said was, "Alma was very special. Charles cherished her."

The inverted *V*s of his dark eyebrows lifted. "I bet that really ticked you off. Or did he keep you around for a little side action when things got dull?"

Her brain ingested the words, rolled them around and tried several times to connect them before she realized what he meant. "You bastard. Don't make assumptions about my life. You don't have a clue what Charles and I felt for each other. Oh, excuse me—" she nodded graciously as if something had just occurred to her "—I forgot. You're better at assumptions than you are at commitments."

She was standing almost toe-to-toe with him now, although it was hard to look him in the eye without tilting her head backward since he was so much taller than she. The dark thing in his eyes flickered and flared to life, and she recognized contempt, and a rage as deep as her own.

"Jill?" The husky feminine voice carried a note of worry. "What's wrong?"

Jillian turned. Her sister Marina was rushing toward her, practically dragging her husband Ben along in her wake.

Jillian moved toward her, taking her hands and slowing her to a halt. "Nothing's wrong." She made an effort to focus. "Except that we're standing at a funeral for two people who never should have died so young." She heaved a sigh, aware that Dax was still behind her, but planning to ignore him. Permanently.

"Marina. Have I changed that much?" She should have known Dax wouldn't slink away quietly. No such luck. He came up beside them and took Marina's hands from Jillian's, a smile so much warmer than the hateful greeting Jillian had received sliding across his tanned features that she blinked and stared.

Then she realized her sister was looking at her for help, her pretty face clouded by the knowledge that this was someone she should know.

"Um, Marina, this is Dax Piersall, Charles's brother."

Dax was already opening his mouth to ask a question when she turned to him. "Marina was in an accident a few years ago that caused her to forget some things. She doesn't remember much of her childhood."

"Charles's *brother?*" Marina's wide blue eyes filled with tears as she gripped Dax's hands. "I didn't know Charles had any family. I'm so sorry—"

"Don't be." Dax's words were a whip that halted the flow of words midstream. "We hadn't seen each other in years. We weren't close." He shot a glance at Jillian and an expression very near a sneer distorted his face. "Not like Charles and Jillian were *close.*"

"Stop it, Dax," she said coolly. "You can snipe at me all you like, but at least try not to be a bore to the rest of the world."

There was a flat, dead silence. Then Dax drew a breath and looked at Marina again, and again, Jillian noticed his expression softened. "I'm sorry you don't remember me. We had some good times together when we were kids."

"I'm sorry, too," she said softly. Turning, she drew her husband forward. "This is my husband, Ben Bradford. Ben, Dax Piersall, who apparently is one of my childhood friends."

Jillian's brother-in-law thrust out his hand and gripped Dax's, but she noticed Ben wasn't smiling. Neither was Dax, and the similarities between the two men struck her suddenly. Both were quite tall, strong without being bulky, dark-eyed and black-haired—although Ben's hair was a warmer shade, and there were traces of silver at his temples that Dax hadn't acquired yet. Unless he colored them, she thought nastily.

Both men also exuded an aura of raw power, a force field of some kind of personality energy that other people recognized and deferred to instantly. Except for those who happened to be named Jillian Kerr.

Ben stepped back from the handshake, clearly dismissing Dax. "You'll have to excuse us," he said to Jillian. "I have to get Marina home. She needs to get out of this heat and rest."

Marina rolled her eyes. "'Rest,' he says. The baby will be screaming for another feeding by the time I get home. Oh, yeah, I'll get plenty of rest."

Ben took her hand, grinning now. "We'll see you later," he said to Jill.

"I'm leaving now," she said, seizing the chance to get away from Dax's presence. "I'll walk with you."

But Dax snagged her hand before she could get away, tightening his fingers around hers until it hurt when she tried to pull free. "You can't leave yet. We have some reminiscing to do."

"Let her go," said Ben, stepping forward, his jaw jutting aggressively.

"It's okay, Ben," Jillian said hastily. "Dax and I *do* have some things to discuss." Her heart had done a back flip at the first touch of his firm, warm skin against hers, and her body quickened in anticipation. She might hate him, but he still had the power to move her physically.

Trying not to show it, she tested his grip, but he still didn't let her go. She didn't want to be touching him, and he knew it. But she wasn't going to let him intimidate her. She might as well show him right off that she was capable of giving as good as she got, she decided with perverse satisfaction.

Stepping close, she pressed her body against him, sliding her free hand up his chest to toy with his tie. Even though she had braced herself for the contact, she had to close her eyes to hide the impact of awareness his hard body provoked.

His eyes widened fractionally. Then they narrowed and his hand loosened around hers. He slipped one arm around her in a familiar manner, his hand resting on the swell of her hip, fingers spread wide to hold her firmly against him. The electric sizzle that surged through her at the contact nearly wiped her mind clean.

Concentrating, she forced herself to ignore the small explosions of arousal going off in her system, gathering her words and her wits. "Among the things we need to talk about is Piersall Industries—now that we're the primary stockholders in the company. You two go on."

She never took her gaze from Dax's as she spoke, and though he hid any trace of surprise, she noted the shock in his eyes when she mentioned the business. So he hadn't known Charles had willed her all of his stock in Piersall. But then, she'd only learned about it this morning, so she'd hoped he hadn't heard yet.

She sensed the hesitation in her sister, knew Ben was reluctant to leave her alone with Dax. She also knew Ben's temper. And the protective streak that was a mile wide. If she didn't get rid of him, there were liable to be two men throwing punches in a minute. So she kept the frozen smile in place, waiting until, from the corner of her vision, she saw them turn and start away again.

As soon as they did, she stepped away from Dax, and to her surprise, he let her go. It was a good thing, too. Every inch of her that had been plastered against him was throbbing and she could barely think.

"You leave my sister out of this," she said to him in a fierce tone.

"She really doesn't remember me, does she?"

"She doesn't remember *anything* from before her accident," Jillian said. "Lucky girl. I'd trade places with her in a heartbeat." Before he could speak again, she went on. "Really, Dax, you should have let me know you were coming. I'd have arranged a little party if I'd known. Invited every other loser in town."

"You've changed," he said. "The old Jillian was a sweetheart, not a sidewinder."

She hated the way he was looking her over, like she was one of the Arabian mares his family had owned when they were growing up. "Of course I've changed," she said briskly, impersonally. She'd die before she'd acknowledge the zing of hurt that verbal arrow produced. "I'm a grown woman with a business and a life to manage."

"Kids' Place."

Her shock had to show, and the uneasiness telling her there was trouble ahead flared even higher. "How do you know about my store? I thought you said you just came to town."

He smiled, and the deadly anger in his eyes did make her step back this time. "I made it my business to know everything there is to know about you, honey-bunch."

"Not everything, since you apparently didn't know about the stock."

"Jill!" A man's voice called to her and she turned, concentrating on forcing a warm smile into place.

"How are you, honey?" Roger Wingerd came toward her and briefly embraced her before drawing back. "I'm going to miss Charles. The Lion's Club's fund-raising committee was his baby. Nobody else can come close to following in his footsteps.''

She nodded, her throat tight as an image of Charles, wearing an apron and flipping pancakes at the annual breakfast, popped up. ''I know.''

Beside her, Dax stirred restively, then thrust his hand forward. ''Dax Piersall.''

Roger's eyes widened as he returned the handshake. ''Roger Wingerd.''

''Roger is the Chief Financial Officer at Piersall,'' Jillian told Dax. ''He and Charles have worked together for almost seven years. Roger probably knew him better than anyone but Alma.'' *Better than you,* was the unspoken message.

Roger appeared oblivious to the tension in the air. ''Sorry about your loss. Charles was one of a kind.''

''He certainly was,'' Dax muttered under his breath.

Jillian ignored him, keeping her gaze fixed on Roger. ''Are we still on for Thursday night?''

Roger nodded. ''I was hoping so, but I'll understand if you don't feel like going out.''

''By then, I'll be all right,'' she assured him, delighting in the chance to throw her life-style in Dax's face. ''Pick me up—''

''She's not free Thursday night. Or any other night.'' The deep voice was clearly audible now, cutting off her words.

Rage rose, practically choking her as she spun to face Dax. ''You have no right to interfere in my life. No right at all.''

But he was looking over her head at Roger and his eyes were telegraphing a primitive message of aggression that belied his sophisticated exterior. If he'd even heard what she'd said, he gave no sign of it. ''You can spread the news. Jillian's permanently out of circulation while I'm in town.''

Roger cast her one swift, questioning glance and she shook her head emphatically. ''He's hallucinating. Again. I'll call you—'' she threw Dax a murderous look ''—once

I straighten out Cro-Magnon Man here on a couple of issues.''

As Roger beat a hasty retreat, she turned on Dax again. "Don't you ever do that again. As far as I'm concerned, our engagement never existed. I don't appreciate you intimidating my friends and antagonizing my family."

Dax shrugged, his eyes unreadable. "It was kind of fun."

"Get out of my life," she said furiously. "You've done it before. You shouldn't have any trouble remembering how to slink out of town."

His jaw tightened as if he was clenching his teeth together, but he glanced at his watch, again as if he hadn't even heard her, and she had to resist the impulse to ball her fist and deck him. Then he lifted his gaze to hers again. "I'm going to be back in your life for quite a while, honeybunch. So you'd better get used to it."

And before she could respond, he stepped past her and strode away.

Four hours later, the last of Charles's and Alma's mourning friends had left the reception hall at the church. Jillian had urged platters of food on their friends, insisting that she would never be able to use it all. She'd comforted more tearful people than she could count, gone through the equivalent of ten boxes of tissues, and shed her high-heeled shoes under a table somewhere.

She'd had five offers to get stinking drunk, two concerned friends who offered to stay the night, and one proposition from a slimy guy who'd said he was a friend of Charles's. The first group was the only one that remotely tempted her.

Leaving the cleanup effort to the bereavement committee from the church, she drove the few miles home and parked in the driveway of her condo. God, she was tired. Every single cell in her body felt bruised; she winced at the effort it took to push open the door and get out. In contrast to her aching body, her mind was numb. It was as though she were wrapped in a thick layer of blankets, the heavy fabric insulating her from reality.

Whatever that was. Reality had taken a vacation the day she got that first frantic phone call from the hysterical housekeeper who had been contacted by the police. There'd been no one else to identify Charles and Alma, and so she'd done it.

They'd died instantly when a drunken driver had slammed into them head-on. There weren't many things in her life that could compare to the horrible reality of examining the mangled remains of two people she loved. No, compared to that, even being dumped by a fiancé seemed more bearable somehow.

Fumbling for her keys in the dark, she stubbed her toe on the step up to her porch and swore. All she wanted to do was to fall into bed and let the world go by for about ten days—

"Wha—?" She gasped as a shadowed figured rose from the single rocking chair. Her heart roared into double-time, and when she recognized the large shape, it only sped up. "Damn it, Dax, you scared me silly."

"Sorry." He didn't sound sorry; only amused.

"Go away." She skirted him, careful not to get too close as she inserted her key in the lock. "I'm tired. You weren't invited."

"I'm inviting myself. We have a lot to discuss." He stepped nearer, and she could see his eyes gleaming in the dim light. "Have dinner with me. Tomorrow night. I'll pick you up at seven."

"Only in your dreams, big boy." She shook her head and tried to hide the quivering in her voice. If he just wouldn't stand so darn close! "I have plans for tomorrow night. And I'm sure my calendar is full up until, oh, about the year twenty-fifty. Sorry, no time for you."

She turned the key and turned her back on him.

"Your lease for Kids' Place is up next month."

The calm, confident words halted her in mid-motion and she paused. "You did your homework."

"Sugar's is up in November. So is The Cotton Gin's."

So much for trying to be clever. "And that means what, exactly, to me?" she demanded. Sugar's and The Cotton Gin were two of the other stores in the shopping center where Kids' Place was located.

"It means," said Dax, "that you're talking to the new owner of the Downington Plaza. The owner who can refuse to renew certain leases if he so chooses."

It was too much, coming on the heels of the horrendous day she'd endured, and her battered brain refused to comprehend his meaning. Weakly, she sank into the rocker he'd vacated as the implications of his words sank into her head. He *owned* her building. And he would refuse to renew her lease. "Why?" she asked quietly, swallowing the note of pain. "Why are you doing this to me? You've done enough already—"

"*I've* done enough?" The words were a volcanic explosion and she shrank back at the rage spewing forth. "What about what *you* did? How do you think I felt, discovering my fiancée and my only brother were screwing around behind my back? How do you think I felt, coming face to face with the two of you sharing declarations of love in the same bed *I'd* been in a few hours before?" He leaned down and put both hands on the rocker's arms, trapping her against the chair back. "Too damn bad for you I came home early that evening, and pretty damn lucky for me. At least I discovered what a little bitch you are before you got a wedding ring on your finger."

The silence that crept into the void left behind his words crackled with the remains of his anger. Their faces were inches apart, and she hoped her expression was as hostile as his was. She was too busy controlling her shaking limbs to be sure.

With a sound of disgust, Dax pushed away from the

rocker. Turning his back to her, he leaned an arm against the brick wall, resting his bent head against it.

And, despite the fear and fury warring inside her, a part of her longed to go to him and rub the tension from his shoulders, smooth the vertical lines that had formed between his brows, rock him until the sorrow in his heart subsided.

She needed to have her head examined.

Reaching for the most disdainful voice she could muster, she said, "So let me be sure I have this straight. I go to dinner with you tomorrow night or you throw my business and those of several other innocent people out of their stores?"

His shoulders straightened. "If that's what it takes." He turned to face her, but she couldn't see his expression in the darkness. "I met with the family attorney after the funeral. He told me Charles did indeed leave you his shares." There was bitterness in his tone. "Payment for services rendered?"

She hissed in a breath, grabbed her temper before it got away, and counted to ten. "I have no earthly idea why Charles left that stock to me. It would have gone to Alma if she'd survived him, you know." Her voice shook unexpectedly as an image of Charles's practical, soft and gentle little wife appeared in her head.

There was a tense silence. She could practically feel the rage emanating from him. But all he said was, "Since you're now a company stockholder, you need to know that Piersall Industries is in trouble."

"What do you mean, 'in trouble'?" She was cautious, wondering what kind of trap this was.

"In trouble," he repeated. He stepped out of the deepest shadows and his eyes were deadly serious. "That stock you hold won't be worth the paper it's printed on if something isn't done to turn Piersall around."

"Something like what?" She didn't care about the stock, nor the profits from it; she'd succeeded in making her life comfortable without it so far. But as a businesswoman, the idea of a company closing, putting who knew how many people out of work, was anathema to her. And this was the only link she had now with Charles; she wasn't ready to toss it aside, even to spite Dax.

Without answering her question, he said, "Tomorrow night. Seven. Dress is casual." He stepped over to her door and twisted the key, opening the door before withdrawing the keys and tossing them into her lap. "Go to bed. You look like hell."

She couldn't just sit there and take more of his insults; it had been a long time since she'd allowed any man to get the better of her. "If I look like hell, it's from having the misfortune to be in the same city with you again."

She was still sitting in the rocker when he turned the corner and vanished into the parking lot.

Two

She can still wrap you up in more knots than a sailor could, Dax thought. He leaned his head against the back of his seat, putting off the moment of ringing Jillian's doorbell and seeing the ice in those blue eyes.

He'd been well-prepared for their first meeting yesterday...he'd thought. Until she'd sprung her little coup on him. He still couldn't believe she controlled twenty-three per cent of the company's voting stock now.

Ever since he'd received the brief, stilted facsimile telling him Charles was dead, he'd imagined that first meeting with her. Dax had been shocked to his shoes when he'd seen Jillian's name on the letterhead; he'd almost conditioned himself to stop thinking of home, and of anyone connected to his past.

Especially her. God, how he'd hated her. It had taken years for him to stop thinking of her every minute, *years,* and with one damned piece of paper, she was back in his

head as if she'd never left. When he'd flown up here from
Atlanta, the man he'd hired to investigate her met him at
the airport with everything he'd dug up. And as he scanned
the doings of Jillian Kerr through the past seven years or
so, he'd known he wasn't going to walk away this time
without wringing some answers out of her. Maybe once he
knew *why* she'd agreed to marry him when she'd obviously
wanted Charles, maybe then he could finally forget.

A few more phone calls had put him in exactly the position he wanted, and he'd strolled off to the funeral yesterday feeling pretty pleased with himself and primed for a
fight. When he'd made his way through the crowd, he'd
been ready to rip her to shreds, exactly the way she'd
ripped his heart out once.

Only he hadn't bargained for the compelling reaction his
body and his emotions had experienced when he sat down
beside her at the service. He hadn't gotten a good look at
her face right away, and it was just as well. He'd been so
fixated on the sight of her slender thighs beneath the short
black skirt, and the way she'd kept her legs pasted together,
with her long, narrow feet in their elegant, unsuitable shoes
cuddled side by side on the ground, that he couldn't have
spoken if he'd had to. Memories had swamped him. He
could still see her long, slender body, feel the way she'd
yielded beneath him, hear the sweet little whimpers she
made when he was touching her.

It had taken him every minute of the rest of that eulogy
to battle the need back into submission, to keep his hands
from reaching out and yanking her against him. And then,
when she'd stood and he'd looked directly at her for the
first time, he'd been poleaxed by her glowing, youthful ap-
pearance. The woman was thirty-two years old, for God's
sake. He knew she'd been around the block more times
than a kid on a new bike, and yet she still looked fresh as
a flower on a dewy morning.

She'd barely seemed to notice him; he had felt her grief and the determined way she was clinging to control. It only served to enrage him all over again. Apparently, she'd stayed close to Charles all these years; Dax doubted she'd be so emotional if he were the one in that coffin.

That coffin. Regret halted his tumbling thoughts. Somehow, he'd always assumed he and Charles would speak again some day. Dax could never forgive Jillian, but Charles was another story.

He, Dax, knew firsthand just how seductive and irresistible she could be. As a hormone-laden kid, he'd been deeply, profoundly jealous of Charles and the special connections his brother had shared with her. Charles and Jillian were thick as thieves, had been since they were old enough to ride their bikes up and down the hill from one house to the other. They touched each other casually, easily, and even though she'd belonged to Dax since their first kiss, she and Charles had some unspoken relationship that didn't include him. Their closeness had bothered him more than he'd wanted to admit, even to himself.

Still, he wished he had taken the time to contact Charles during these recent years, when his brother had popped into his mind more and more frequently. He hadn't even come home for their mother's funeral four years ago, a move he still regretted. And he'd fully intended to get back in touch with Charles. He'd considered it a dozen times, had told himself tomorrow would be time enough. Now tomorrow had arrived, but time had run out.

Charles…his baby brother. Gone. In his mind's eye, Dax watched Jillian lay a yellow rose atop the white coffin. A numbing regret swept over him. He'd missed Charles these past few years.

And he'd have liked to have met his brother's wife. He would have applauded anyone who could steal Charles out from under Jillian's nose.

He unfolded himself from the sleek little Beamer that had been left at the house since his mother's death and walked to her door. She opened it after the first ring, as if she'd been standing on the other side waiting on him. Good. He hoped she'd stood there a while.

The punch of awareness slammed into him again at the sight of that angelic face and even though he'd been expecting it, he still could only stare for a moment, drinking in the porcelain beauty that had once been his. She was wearing a fairly sedate, un-Jillian-like twin set and stylish trousers. She'd always dressed to entice, to arouse...before. Of course, that could have changed over the years.

He recalled the curve-hugging black suit she'd worn to the funeral, the suit with the tight skirt that had shown off her slender little butt and lots of long, slim leg. He'd been watching from his car when she'd been helped out of the hearse by two exceedingly attentive men, and he'd endured the painful twist in his gut when she'd clung to one of them as she started across the cemetery. And he'd been mildly surprised to note that her figure had looked every bit as good as he remembered...though ''surprise'' hadn't been the primary feeling he'd experienced.

And afterwards, when he'd introduced himself to her family, he'd been shocked as hell when she'd deliberately closed the space between them and pressed herself against his side as if they were intimate companions who touched each other every day. Even though he knew she'd done it to head off more hard words between him and her overbearing brother-in-law, he hadn't been able to prevent himself from touching her once he'd recovered his wits. He'd slid a hand around her still-slender waist and checked out the firm curve of her hip, and it had been all he could do to stand there when all he wanted was to pull her against him and fill his hands with her.

He suspected that this sudden switch to conservative

clothing was for his benefit. She'd probably had to run out and buy it today.

The idea made him smile as he started forward—but she blocked his way. "I'm ready."

That was it. No greeting, no civil conversation. The imp of perversity that she brought out in him popped up, and he merely stood there, blocking *her* way, now. "Invite me in."

"No. You asked me to dinner. Let's go."

"Come on, honey-bunch." He used the endearment deliberately, and her eyelids fluttered once, a subtle flinch that he might have missed if he hadn't been looking for it. He'd noticed yesterday that the expression he'd once used with tenderness got her back up like a threatened cat's. "It's only natural that I want to see how my former fiancée is living. After all, if we'd married, I'd have been saddled with your taste in furnishings for life." He put his hands on her waist and set her aside, striding into the foyer of her condo, where he made a show of looking around. But his body was doing its Jillian-thing again, and he had to take a few deep breaths to calm the shaky feeling that touching her had produced in his gut. His fingers tingled and his blood felt as if it was racing through his veins. And unfortunately, there wasn't a lot he could do about the heavy stirring in the part of his body that hadn't listened when he told himself it was over with her.

This really sucked. He'd met dozens—no, *hundreds* of beautiful, sexy women over the years. And not one of them could arouse even a fraction of the desire that rode him when he so much as thought about Jillian.

"I'd really like to get this over with. I have to work tomorrow."

"At your store." Leisurely, he strolled through a stark, white kitchen that looked as if it didn't get much use. The only personal touches were a couple of pictures of children—Marina's?—held on the refrigerator with magnets, and a clumsily painted clay bowl that looked like it had been made by a child. The other items on display looked like they'd been placed there by a decorator for effect. He ran a finger over a blue glazed bowl with apples in it, mildly surprised when he realized the apples were real.

He inspected the dining room, with its smoked glass table and chrome-and-leather chairs. The room was dominated by a huge painting of... "What is that?"

She'd been trailing after him, looking distinctly pouty and disgruntled. At his words, a small smile curled the edges of her lips up in amusement. "It's a painting."

He gave her a narrow-eyed look.

She raised both palms and shrugged. "I don't know what it is. Some days, it looks like a tiger wearing green socks, other days it resembles a garden of orange lilies. Vaguely. It was a gift from an artist and I don't want to hurt his feelings."

"His?" He mentally kicked himself the moment the word came out. It certainly wasn't what he'd intended to say. What *had* he intended to say, anyway?

Jillian crossed her arms and leaned back against the door frame. "Yes, *his,* as in male, man, masculine gender. Believe it or not, Dax, I've had a life of my own since your exit, complete with a few—gasp!—relationships along the way."

He ignored the sarcasm, heading into the next room, which must be her formal living room. An enormous baby grand occupied the alcove in the corner, and sheet music for a complicated arrangement of the love theme from *Titanic* was open above the keys. Jillian had loved to play, he remembered. Apparently, at least that hadn't changed. He wandered past the piano to where a tasteful grouping of white love seats and chairs were set before a brass-screened fireplace with white marble columns.

Who did she share that love seat with now? Rationally, he knew she had had no reason to suspend her life after he'd left, but when he thought about Jillian with another man, his irrational side wanted to smash a few pieces of her Lladro collection against the far wall.

A group of brass-framed photos displayed on the mantel caught his eye, and he went closer. Her sister's family smiled contentedly into the camera in the first one. There was a dark-haired little girl cradled in Ben Bradshaw's arm and an obviously pregnant Marina glowed with happiness. Regret rose at the cozy family scene, and he swallowed it, moving on to the next image. Slightly behind the first, a second photo showed Marina snuggled against a big blond guy.

Before he could voice a question, Jillian said, "That was her first husband. He was killed in the accident." There was a soft, sad note in her voice that made him want to reach out and cuddle her, comfort her, but he resisted such a stupid impulse.

The third photo arrested his attention, as did two others following it. The photographer apparently had been waiting for the shot, because the three photos were a sequence. In the first, taken near someone's pool on a bright, sunny day, an enormous hulk of a guy in nothing but a pair of blue denim cutoffs that bared bulging biceps and thighs like tree trunks was sneaking up behind Jillian. Meanwhile, another broad-shouldered dark-haired man in swim trunks stood with his arm around her naked waist. She was wearing what had to be the skimpiest bikini on the East Coast and even though the man's hand was only splayed against her back, Dax's blood pressure rose.

In the second photo, the Hulk had snatched her off her feet and was holding her cradled against his chest as he stood on the edge of the pool. He was grinning like the Cheshire cat. Jillian had his ears in her hands, tugging, her head thrown back and her mouth open in a scream. The third was a marvelous action shot of the pair in midair, free-falling into the pool as sprays of water froze forever for the camera's lens.

Jillian had moved up beside him. She reached up to trace a delicate finger over the glass, sliding around the outline of the big man. She heaved an exaggerated sigh.

He couldn't take it, even though he knew she was baiting him. "Someone special?"

"Two someones," she corrected, smiling fondly at the photo. "Other than my brother-in-law, Jack and Ronan are the men I love most in the world. Even when they conspire to throw me into the pool."

He gritted his teeth, aware that if he moved right now, it only would be far enough to get his hands around her unfaithful throat. "You never were satisfied with just one of anything." He hadn't meant the words in an intimate sense, but as he glanced at her, he suddenly realized they applied to their shared past in another way.

And in the sudden aura of awareness that the words dropped over them, he saw in her eyes that she was thinking the same thing he was. Their lovemaking had always been intense and primitive, and they'd both been young, healthy, in love with lust when they'd been together. A single episode of sex had never been enough for her. As if she were speaking, he could hear her husky voice urging him on and on, begging him for more and more, and protesting that she really *couldn't* without meaning it when he moved over her, giving her a second satisfaction only moments after the first.

He looked at her lips. They were slightly parted, the edges of her perfect teeth—courtesy of the braces he still remembered—showing. She was breathing in quick, shallow gulps. He could practically smell the scent of her arousal, and the erection that had been teasing him since she opened the door roared to full, throbbing life. His hand reached for hers, their gazes locking in a desperate, wordless exchange. Taking her small hand in his, he carried it to his chest.

She sucked in a strangled breath, her eyes darting to their hands—

And the tidal wave of sudden, rigid-muscled, bodyshaking rage that possessed him when he thought about her running straight from his arms into those of his brother blasted through him without warning, knocking down any fragile barriers he'd sandbagged against it.

"How many men have those hands touched?" he demanded, as he flung her hand from him.

For an instant, he thought he saw anguish pass over her features. Then, if it had ever been there at all, the desperate emotion in her eyes vanished. Tossing her head to throw back her hair, she smiled. "Dozens. And every single one of them tells me I'm the best thing he's ever known."

He could kill her. *He really could kill her.*

Reading his eyes correctly, she hastily stepped back. But she just couldn't shut that smart mouth of hers. "You asked for that, Dax. You know you did." She paused, and weariness drew at her pretty face; again, for a moment, she looked so sad that a little part of his heart almost reached out for her before he shoved it back into hiding. "If I told you the truth, you'd think I was lying, anyway."

"You aren't capable of telling the truth," he snarled. *Truth? What truth?*

In self-preservation, he transferred his attention to the last photo.

And was shocked speechless for a moment. It was a close-up of Jillian. She was cradling an infant in her arms, a newborn whose blond fuzz barely dusted the tiny head. She was holding the child up close to her, looking into its face, and the tenderness in her expression dug into him like a sharp blade. His hands were shaking and he shoved them into his pockets. *Was it hers? Where was it?* The sight sent sharp arrows of pain through him again.

That should have been my child.

But she hadn't loved him enough to have his babies.

As if she'd followed his thoughts, she said quietly, "That's my friend Deirdre's first child. He's a whole lot bigger and a *whole* lot livelier now, but he sure was precious then."

His shoulders slumped as the tension leached out of him, and with a small shake of his head for what should have been and never would be, he gave up the inspection and escorted her out the door.

As Dax drove up the hill and pulled into the circular driveway fronting Charles and Alma's house—or was it Dax's now?—Jillian steeled herself. The last time she'd been here had been the day after they'd died, when the funeral director had asked her to pick out clothing in which the couple could be buried. God save her from ever having to choose another loved one's final attire.

"Why are we stopping here?"

Dax gave her an unreadable glance as he killed the engine. "We're dining here."

She stared at him a minute. "I hope you're joking."

He looked puzzled. "Do I look like I'm joking?"

She couldn't eat here. No. Absolutely no way. "Dax...the past few times I've been in this house haven't exactly been easy moments for me. I thought you meant we were eating out or I'd never have agreed to come with you."

He uncoiled himself from the driver's seat and came around the car to open her door. "Get out." His voice was clipped.

He was determined to make her life a living hell, she

thought in resentment. She never should have told him coming to the house bothered her; he was far to quick to seize on things and rub them into her skin.

"Get out or I'll get you out." The menace in his voice convinced her he meant it.

Slowly, she swung her legs out of the car and stood, ignoring the hand he extended, and walked up the wide, shallow flagstone steps before he could touch her.

Following her up, he reached around her to open the door. As he turned the knob, he hesitated and looked down at her.

She averted her eyes, refusing to give him the satisfaction of seeing the pain she was feeling, and after a moment, he pushed the door inward and she preceded him into the spacious foyer. Mrs. Bowley, the housekeeper who'd been there since they were small, bustled through the swinging door from the kitchen and hurried down the hall, wiping her hands on her apron.

"Jillian!" The older woman enfolded her in a warm, cinnamon-y smelling embrace that catapulted her back in time. Funny how some smells always made you remember certain things. Mrs. Bowley's scent always relaxed her and gave her the warm, secure feelings she'd known in childhood. When the housekeeper stepped back, her faded blue eyes were swimming with tears. "How are you, honey?"

"I'm fine." She gripped Mrs. Bowley's hands. "I've been worried about you. Have you been all right?"

The housekeeper gave her a watery smile. "It's been hard. I keep expecting Miss Alma to come flying down the steps, or Charles to come out of his study with his nose buried in the paper."

"I'm sure." Jillian draped an arm around her sloping shoulders. "I can't quite accept it yet, either."

"Having Dax come home has been wonderful. And of course, there's—"

"Mrs. Bowley." Dax's voice was warm but firm. "Could you please bring us the hors d'oeuvres?"

"Right away, dear." The older woman gave Jillian one last fond smile as she turned away.

Dax crossed the hall and opened the door of Charles's study. Only she supposed it was *his* study now. She looked at him, uncomprehending, before she realized he wanted her to go into that room, rather than into the parlor opposite it, where guests were usually entertained. Or at least, where Charles, and Dax's parents before him, had entertained. It was difficult to remember that this was Dax's home now.

As she passed him and entered the room, he asked, "Would you like a drink?"

"A glass of sherry would be nice," she said. He disappeared again, and she dropped her purse in a wing chair as she idly walked to the window and pulled back the heavy drapes. She couldn't stand to sit in here in the dark, and it was still light outside. Perching on the wide ledge, she stared at the familiar scene without really seeing it.

Crossing her arms, she lifted each of her hands to the opposite shoulder and massaged her neck for a moment. If she spent much more time in Dax's company, she was going to need a massage therapist on a permanent basis.

He returned with her drink, and one of his own, and walked across the rug to hand it to her. At the same moment, Mrs. Bowley bustled in with a small tray. She deposited it on the table beside Jillian and left again.

As he switched on the floor lamp behind the desk, Dax said, "Come sit down. There are some things I want to ask you about."

She frowned as she settled into the wing chair, trying to ignore the way his casual olive pants pulled across his thighs when he propped one hip on the edge of the massive cherry desk. Across his definitely-all-man thighs. She swallowed. She should have smacked his face when he'd taken her hand in her condo.

Why hadn't she? She couldn't explain it, even to herself. It was as if she'd lost all willpower, all independent thought, when he'd looked at her with those lazy, sexy eyes of his. They'd told her, without words, that he was remembering how wild and incredible their lovemaking had been. And she'd felt her body softening, yearning for him even though she knew he despised her.

And she despised him, of course.

But it stung her pride that he'd been the one to move away. He'd been quick to spoil the magic in the moment, too, and old hurt rose in her throat. Why was he so determined to think the worst of her? It struck her that he'd been just as determined to condemn her seven years ago. It was almost as if he *wanted* to believe she was a woman with fewer morals than the owner of the infamous Chicken Ranch.

"What do you know about Piersall Industries?" The curt question scattered her whirling thoughts, and she had to consider it for a minute.

"Other than the fact that it's your family's business that manufactures steel beams for construction?" She shrugged. "Not much. If you're hoping I'll walk you through the family finances, you're out of luck." And she couldn't resist adding, "Charles and I didn't talk much about business when we were together."

"Don't be childish," he told her. "You don't need to prove anything to me. I already know about your affection for my brother. What I want to know is whether or not you can explain to me how Charles dug this company into a hole so deep I may not be able to get it out."

She had been staring at him angrily until his last words penetrated, and she sat up straighter, unable to believe her ears. "What? You must have misread something. The company should be in great shape. Charles was always looking for charitable causes that would help offset the chunk of change the IRS demands. He's been one of Baltimore's most generous patrons of a number of community projects.''

Dax smiled grimly. ''Yeah? Well, it looks like he's been a little too magnanimous. Although it'll be a while before I know for sure. He seems to have been the world's worst record-keeper.''

''He hated that end of it,'' she admitted. ''Charles was a people person, remember? But he had employees to manage the finances. Have you talked with Roger Wingerd about this?''

''Not yet. I wanted to get familiar with the current setup before I started questioning people.'' Dax rubbed the back of his neck as he picked up a thick sheaf of papers and handed them to her. ''You probably won't understand this, but it's a copy of the quarterly financial report. It's not good.''

''I studied accounting, remember?'' she said examining the numbers with growing dread. ''I've kept my C.P.A. certification even though I don't practice any more.''

''Any more?''

She looked up, shooting him a grim smile. ''I worked for Arthur Andersen for almost five years before Marina and I opened our store.''

One black eyebrow rose. ''I'm impressed.'' But his tone was mocking.

Refusing to respond in kind, she said, ''Thank you.'' Then she waved the report at him, concern mounting. ''I'd have to see a lot more than this to get the whole picture, but it does look as if Piersall is in trouble.''

''In trouble?'' Dax snorted. ''If something isn't done, this company will have to declare bankruptcy by the end of the year.''

She was shocked and for a minute she simply gaped at him. "My God, Dax. Do you realize how many people will lose their jobs if Piersall sinks?"

He pivoted and picked up another piece of paper from the desk top. "Four hundred, more or less, with about ninety per cent of them full-timers who would lose benefits."

"I had no idea," she whispered.

"Apparently, neither did Charles." For once, Dax appeared unconcerned about continuing their verbal battles. "I was hoping you could shed some light on this."

She started to shake her head, and then the light dawned. "No, you weren't." She drained her glass of sherry and set it on the table beside her with a snap. "You didn't see my name on the list of employees, and you wanted to know if I'd been helping Charles to mismanage his funds. You *jerk.*"

Springing out of the chair, she stalked toward the door, but she'd forgotten how fast he could move. He was laughing as he took her elbow and steered her toward the dining room. "Caught by a master of deception. What can I say?" He barely twisted out of the way when she rammed her elbow backward toward his ribs. "Calm down, honeybunch. I don't recall making any accusations."

"Then you had a memory lapse."

"Anyway," he said, staying out of range, "You can relax. I don't think you had anything to do with the company's problems."

"How generous of you," she said bitterly. "You'll have to excuse me for thinking that you assessed my reaction before rendering such a magnanimous opinion."

"But I need you to help me solve them." He went on as if she hadn't spoken. "There's been a little movement of the company's stock in the week since Charles died. Probably normal reaction, but it bears watching. In the meantime, I've been looking over the minutes from recent board meetings and I can't say I'm impressed with the general direction they've been going."

"And naturally, you have a solution." She couldn't resist.

"I do." He picked up his drink and took a slow sip, watching her over the rim of the glass before he spoke again. "But it may not be one that the current board will embrace unless I can force them to yield by outvoting them at the table."

Comprehension began to glimmer in the back of her mind. "Just how much stock do you own, Dax?"

"Together, the family held fifty-one percent," he said. "Now that Charles has left his shares to you, I still control twenty-eight percent."

"So..." She made a show of crossing her legs and settling back in her chair. "Without my votes, you can't be sure of enough support to control the board."

Dax's mouth was a grim line. "No. I can't."

She raised one brow in a mocking manner as she made a production out of recrossing her legs the other way. "Ah. How...interesting."

"'Interesting' isn't quite the word I'd use," he grated. "God, I could kill you. And I could kill Charles for creating this mess if he weren't dead already."

Abruptly, any satisfaction she'd found in the verbal sparring drained away. Sorrow and a profound depression filled her. She'd worked so hard to make a life for herself after Dax had left, and now she felt as if she had moved no farther in time than mere hours from the day he'd gone.

She almost demanded that he take her home then, but she knew it would only give him pleasure to refuse. So when he set his glass on the desk and motioned for her to precede him, she moved ahead of him into the dining room without a protest. There were three places set, and despite her irritation with him, she was touched. She knew Charles and Alma had taken most of their meals in the kitchen with Mrs. Bowley. It was thoughtful of Dax to include her.

As they cleared the doorway, she moved to the far end of the room and through the open French doors. Being so close to him was torture. Half of her wanted to kill him, but the other half...the other half wished in vain that she could walk into his arms and let him touch her with those long magic fingers that wreaked havoc on her system.

A gentle evening breeze wandered across the pretty stone patio. Beyond a green carpet of lawn, the pool reflected evening's approach on its smooth face. The sight of that pool brought memories flooding back...more of the uncomplicated happy moments from childhood, anxious yearnings from adolescence as she wished Dax would notice her in her newest bathing suit, and other memories—giddy, heady, heart-pounding recollections that were better left forgotten.

Would this evening ever end? she thought in despair. They hadn't even eaten yet and already she felt like someone had flayed every inch of her skin with a cat-o'-nine-tails. She turned to move from the view, desperately seeking some innocuous subject that wouldn't carry any more bits of her past.

Dax was standing directly behind her.

She barreled into him with a muffled exclamation of surprise; his hands gripped her upper arms to steady her. But when she automatically tried to step back, he held her against him. His big body, where hers was pressed into it, was achingly familiar and enticingly strange. Her breasts knew the planes of his torso, his hips found their old familiar pillow just below her navel. She sucked in a breath of dismay and delight, her body arrested in motion, quivering with the wondrous feel of his form against hers again.

This was what they'd had between them. Since the first

time he'd taken her into his arms to dance on her seventeenth birthday, they'd had this. She could still remember the look on his face that night, the stunned need that accompanied his body's unmistakable response. And she could remember the helpless, melting feeling she'd known, along with the heady sense of power she'd felt when his lips had descended on hers right there on the dance floor.

"You're too young," he'd growled against her skin. And despite her protests, he'd stayed away, even going to Europe to do his graduate work at a university there. He had never even asked her out until the summer he'd turned twenty-four.

He'd come to her house the day he'd returned from Europe, and they'd dated steadily from that point on. It had been two months before he'd made love to her for the first time. Two *long* months, when the only thing that had saved her virgin state was Dax's self-control. She'd had none. And it was a not-quite-pleasant realization to recognize that she still didn't.

She could have stood there all day. She barely resisted her body's pleas to rub herself against him in surrender. Dignity had no place here. Elemental recognition flowed between them. *Rib of my rib, bone of my bone*—she was his missing half, he was the answer to the unfinished equation in her life.

Above her head, Dax muttered something, and she lifted dazed eyes to his. "What?"

"I said, 'Damn.'" His thumbs lightly rubbed over the soft flesh he had seized to steady her, flesh he had yet to release. His eyes searched hers. "My life would be easier without this."

When he spoke, her gaze moved to watch the fascinating motions of his lips as he formed his words. She knew, with no explanation, exactly what he meant. "A lot easier." She sighed. "Of all the men in the world, why are you the only one?"

"Because you were made for me." His voice was a guttural acknowledgment as his head slowly lowered.

She lifted her face the barest increment, knowing it wasn't smart, unable to resist.

Their lips met. Shivers of wild excitement connected that point of contact with a dozen others, all descending to the junction where her legs met.

In one instant, she forgot every hurtful lesson she'd learned from this man. Her arms came up to his shoulders as he pulled her against him. One big hand swept across her back and the other splayed wide just above the swell of her buttocks. She sank against him in total surrender, a surrender he recognized and accepted without a word passing between them. He couldn't get her any closer to him; her fingers speared into his short hair and cradled his scalp as his tongue renewed every intimate motion, explored every silken corner of her mouth.

She was a twig, carried away in the raging winds of a hurricane; a hapless pebble in the path of an avalanche. When he dragged his mouth down her neck, her head dropped back helplessly, though her hands pressed him to her.

"Do you remember our first time?"

The low words were punctuated with kisses that strayed down over her sweater to the tip of her breast. His hand left her back and came around, sliding surely onto the slight mound that already begged for his attention.

She moaned. "Down by the pool."

A chuckle of breath huffed over her. When he pulled the thin sweater away from her waistband and put his hand beneath it, against her skin, she jumped and moaned. His palm left a trail of heat behind, and as it traveled inexorably upward, she pressed her lips to the black silk of his hair.

"Daddy?"

Dax jerked away from her in one shocking movement, yanking his hands from beneath her clothing and holding her arms in an iron grip. He pivoted, placing his body between Jillian and the doors behind them, and pressed her head into his chest with one strong hand.

Ordinarily, she might have protested. But speech was beyond her.

"Just a minute, Christine." His voice was a deep growl, and she could still feel the hard strength of his desire pressing into her. Tremors began to shudder through her.

But the childish voice came again. "Who *is* that, Daddy?"

Dax sighed and released her. Jillian straightened her clothing with trembling hands. Slowly, she forced herself to turn around.

Dax stepped aside, and if she'd been shocked before, every thought fled now. Shock dribbled ice down her neck, sending goose bumps up her arms, leaving a cold ball of lead in the pit of her stomach. The world swam and she instinctively put out a hand, then snatched it away again when it landed on his forearm.

Distantly, she saw him turn, heard him say, "Christine, this is my friend Jillian."

The child was fair, the straight, shaggy strands as blond as Jillian's own. There was no mistaking her parentage, though. Dax's dark eyes under identical brows, drawn now into a suspicious scowl, studied her resentfully. She had his lean frame as well, though on his child it was going to translate into a killer pair of legs one of these days.

How could it hurt so much? She'd put Dax behind her, buried all her imaginings of a family of her own with the remnants of her love for a man who hadn't trusted her enough to believe in her. Now she realized that in holding herself aloof from the possibilities of another love, she'd been punishing *herself*, not Dax, all these years. *She* was the one who'd been alone for the past seven years, while Dax clearly hadn't spent his life in misery over her.

Her breast heaved; a sob burst out without warning and she only kept another from erupting by clamping one hand over her mouth. Abruptly turning from his daughter, Dax reached for her.

But she reared back as if he were a poisonous snake, continuing to inch her way backward until the cold marble of the low railing around the patio kept her from going farther. He stopped and raised his hands as if to reassure her that he wasn't coming any closer, and she stared at him, futilely battling an agony as deep as she'd known the day he'd stared at her with hot rage and hatred burning in his eyes before he'd walked away forever.

She bowed her head and closed her eyes, taking the deep breaths that had gotten her through Charles's and Alma's funeral and a thousand other moments of despondency over the years.

A self-protective wall slammed down. Blessed numbness descended, and she was grateful. Emotion, feeling, was gone. Nothing could hurt her now. Later, maybe, she'd think of this, but right now all she prayed for was the fortitude to deflect this shattering blow that threatened to break her into a thousand shards of desolation.

Summoning what she hoped looked remotely like a smile, she walked toward the little girl. As she extended her hand like an automaton, she gave Dax a wide berth. "I'm Jillian Kerr."

The child stared at the hand as if she wasn't sure what to do with it. Finally, she put out her own and dutifully shook Jillian's hand. "I'm Christine."

It was slightly sullen, but Jillian barely registered the tone. "I knew your father when we were kids, even younger than you are. And despite what you just saw, we aren't really friends at all. We had some business to discuss and I'm going now.''

Slipping past the child—Christine—she made her way out of the dining room *with its three place settings* and walked directly to the hall table. She picked up the phone and called a cab, telling them she'd pay double fare for immediate pickup.

As she opened the heavy front door, she heard Dax call her name. She closed the door gently and kept going. She was almost at the end of the circular driveway when he caught up to her. Walking beside her, he said, ''Jillian?''

She didn't respond. She couldn't. Tears beat at the backs of her eyes; every ounce of her willpower was directed at holding them back. Silently, she concentrated on the meaningless task of counting her measured steps. As she turned left, she started down the street in the direction she knew the cab would be coming.

''Jillian, we have to talk.''

She walked on, putting a hand to her mouth when her breath hitched and another sob threatened.

''You can't walk home, honey. Let me drive you home.'' His voice was surprisingly gentle, but she supposed he could afford to be gentle now.

The cab turned the corner at the bottom of the hill. She stopped to wait for it.

Dax stopped, too, stepping in front of her. ''I meant to tell you about Christine. I wanted you to meet her this evening but not—''

''And I've met her.'' Her eyes focused on him, and she reached for the imaginary wall she envisioned between them. ''If you came back here to punish me, Dax, consider the job done.'' Even she could hear the distress she couldn't quite control in her shaking voice. ''If I had one wish, I'd wish that you were the Piersall who'd been in that car last week.''

His features went from concern to stone-solid stoicism. The cab slowed to a stop at her hail and she opened the door and slid into the back seat while he watched with clenched fists. As she lay her head against the seat back, she gave the driver her address and concentrated anew on forcing back the tears.

Three

Dax sat on the edge of the pool, staring down into the water without really seeing it. It was long past nightfall and his butt was getting tired of the concrete, and still he sat. Trying to make some sense of his life.

He was still shaken by Jillian's reaction to his daughter earlier in the evening. And as the water rippled and beckoned around his calves, he wondered how everything could have gone so wrong. They'd been happy once.

From the first time he'd kissed her to the day he'd caught her in bed with his own brother, they'd been happy. At least, he thought they had been. And damn her eyes, he'd never met another woman who could take her place. Not in his heart, because he wasn't stupid—one lesson had been enough. But even someone he could enjoy enough to share his life with. It wasn't as if he'd had a choice with Libby. They'd married to give Christine legitimacy, but they'd hardly enjoyed their life together.

But in all honesty, he couldn't blame his ex-wife. She'd never had a chance against his memories. He sighed, a bitter sound on the mild night air. It would be nice, *really* nice, if just once, when he was in bed with a woman, he didn't wish it were Jillian beneath him, around him. He might have been able to block her out of his waking thoughts, but she'd haunted his dreams for years.

Memories of her laughing eyes, the flash of her teasing smile, taunted his aching mind. He'd thought of her as a little sister, albeit a rather annoying one, when he was a kid. Marina had been closer to his age and they'd hung out together a lot until high school, when they'd begun to date different people. He'd always marveled at the differences between the two girls. Physically, they could have been twins if they were the same size. Marina was several inches taller than Jillian, but they'd both had that face that stopped boys in their tracks and the long, slim body that knocked them to their knees.

Their personalities, though, couldn't have been more different if they'd been born on separate planets. Marina was calm, Jillian was lively. Marina was quiet; Jillian was gregarious. Marina was even-tempered; Jillian was exuberant and bouncy—or a raging storm. With Jillian, there was no in-between. You either got kissed or killed.

Marina exuded genteel elegance, her clothing always attractive but restrained. But vivacious Jillian couldn't walk into a room without every man in the place taking note of her seductive aura. Which was usually enhanced, he thought sourly, by her, ''Notice me,'' clothing.

At the funeral, a part of him had wanted to wrap his jacket around that too-short skirt and those too-long legs that every man there had been eyeing when their wives' backs were turned. Another part of him had enjoyed the view.

Why couldn't he have had the hots for Marina? She was

his age, his friend, but he'd never felt more than an appreciative twinge of enjoyment for her. Jillian, on the other hand... From the time she was about fourteen, when Jillian came around, his adolescent self had practically quivered with lust. Not a lot different from now, he thought wryly. He could hate her for that alone.

He dipped a hand into the cool water. The very first time he'd made love to her, they'd been beside this pool, lying in the cool grass just off the apron. God, his father would have killed him. And hers would have cut him into small pieces for the barbecue pit. It was an uncomfortable thought, and his fatherly ire rose immediately as he imagined himself in the same situation. Amazing what a few decades could do to your perception.

Of course, he hadn't thought of that at the time. No, all he'd thought about was getting that body-hugging bathing suit off her. They had been dating for two months, since the very day he'd come home early from his year in Europe because she was all he could think of. Since he'd come back, they had spent every available minute together. And although they'd steamed up the windows in his car more than a few times, he'd always backed off when she stopped him. Half the time *he* was the one who stopped. He'd decided to wait until he could ask her to marry him and get a ring on that flirty little finger. Every time they resisted temptation and the yearnings of young, hot blood, he felt pretty damned noble about the sacrifice.

But on the night of her sister's twenty-third birthday, he'd forgotten every promise he'd made to himself.

Her folks had had a birthday supper for Marina, with a few of the girls' mutual friends. Afterward, the whole group had gone swimming up at his house, but one by one, they'd gone home, until only he and Jillian, and Marina and her date, had remained.

And then those two had gone, leaving Jillian and him

alone. He remembered how charged his body had gotten when he'd realized that they were going to be *alone*. They hardly ever spent time alone, partly because she was just too damned tempting, and partly because they went practically everywhere with their small circle of friends, which included his brother and her sister.

As Marina disappeared up the path toward the driveway, Jillian had splashed water in his face, laughing. "Race you."

He'd laughed, too. "When are you going to realize you'll never beat me?"

She'd stuck out her tongue, tagged the wall and taken off. He'd quickly followed, overtaking her with his more powerful strokes just before they reached the shallow end of the pool. He'd grabbed her ankle and dragged her to him as she squealed and wriggled, and he'd wrapped his arms tightly around her, to hold her still as well as—okay, admit it—to cop a feel.

He'd gotten hard the moment he touched her.

The unexpected privacy was a potent aphrodisiac, the knowledge that they were alone sending lusty images dancing through his head. When she'd slid her arms around his neck and pressed her pert, pretty breasts against him, he'd gone wild.

And she hadn't been far behind him. They'd stroked, touched, explored. Groaned, sighed and startled at the sensation of hands on throbbing flesh.

"Dax?" she whispered.

"What?" He had managed to get the little racing suit down to her waist and was suckling a breast, while her hands fluttered up and down over his shoulders as she sagged against him.

"Please, will you...can we...*do it?*"

The stammered question brought his head up. He looked down at her, nestled in his arms, her tightly budded nipples pressing into the hair furring his chest, and his body answered for him. But he'd hesitated, as his conscience reminded him of his promises to himself. His response was a compromise. "We could, but we don't have to. We can just...play."

And then he was lost as she looked up at him, pressed herself even more closely against him, so that his erection was pressed hard against her belly. "But I want to. Make me yours."

Blood rushed to his head. He carried her up the steps and out of the pool, and set her on her feet only long enough to spread out a towel on the grass in the dark shadows beside the pool. Moments later, he had her naked and though he'd touched practically every part of that seductive young body before, seeing her nude, spread out before him with her arms reaching up, made him shake with lust.

He was so hard that getting his own clothes off was agony, and he didn't given her nearly the time and attention he should have. Still, she wrapped her legs around him even as she winced at the discomfort, and responded to his wild kisses fervently as he stroked steadily to his own satisfaction, blind to everything but the need driving him.

It had taken them a few months to figure out how to make it fun for her, and he'd gotten better at waiting for her to join him in her own pleasure. After that, she'd been more woman than any man deserved, and he'd gotten plenty of practice trying to keep up with her.

Shifting his butt on the edge of the pool again, Dax pulled his swimming trunks into a more comfortable position around the arousal that the memories had brought. He rubbed the back of his neck with one hand, then scrubbed both hands over his face. *What the hell had happened to them?*

Suddenly, his trip through the past vanished and he remembered, with a clarity he didn't particularly want, what had happened when Christine appeared.

Arousal died a quick death at *that* memory. What he wanted to find out was what in God's name had been going on in Jillian's head. Correct that last: he *needed* to find out.

There was no mistaking the devastation that had ripped through her when she first saw his daughter. In those first unguarded moments, he'd watched myriad expressions chase each other across her face: shock, disbelief, recognition, incredulity, quickly followed by a hefty hit of agony she couldn't cover. Her eyelids had fluttered and he'd thought for a moment his indestructible Jillian might just faint.

When he'd reached for her, the reaction he got was damn near as shocking as her silent pain. She'd backed away from him, almost in panic, her face drained of all color and her eyes wide and hunted. She'd scared the hell out of him—he'd been certain she was going to back right over the railing.

The message had been clear. Even so, he might have ignored the Do Not Touch signs, except that she looked so fragile and damaged that he couldn't bring himself to hurt her more.

And he had hurt her, of that he was sure. But it wasn't intentional. Just like that damned kiss hadn't been intentional. He was going to tell her about Christine right before dinner, before his daughter came in, but talking had quickly dropped to the bottom of the list of things he wanted to do with Jillian. *Thinking* had been low on the list, too.

He'd initially been as shocked as she to hear that voice interrupt the best thing that had happened to him in…a while. No way was he going to think about the implications of how good she'd felt in his arms. Apparently, she'd felt better in his brother's arms.

The thought didn't bring the usual red mist of rage; Jillian's words were still ringing in his head. *If you came back here to punish me, Dax, consider the job done.*

She'd looked every bit as sick as he'd felt seven years ago, as if she'd just received a gut-punch and was struggling not to throw up. He'd wanted to punish her, to hurt her, true. But he had succeeded too well; the intensity of the pain that had torn her apart in front of his eyes had left the foul taste of a hollow victory in his mouth.

Only hours ago, he'd had a flash of the furious rage which had propelled him clear to Georgia all those years ago. But he couldn't summon up more than a weary regret at the moment. Maybe his successful quest for vengeance had been satisfied.

Though he hated to think he was that petty, that shallow. He hadn't thought clearly since he'd stood in the hallway outside her bedroom door listening to his brother tell her how much he loved her. Now he could see; the murky feelings swirling in his head had settled.

He knew instinctively that she'd never accept his apology. Not after the way she'd reeled and nearly fallen to pieces in front of him. Her nemesis.

But then she'd done something incredible. Something a lot of strong men would never be capable of after a body blow that knocked the wind clear out of them. Just when he thought she was going to dissolve right there in front of him, she'd regrouped. He'd watched her withdraw, hide herself away somewhere in that complicated brain of hers, and silently do some kind of deep meditation. When she looked up again, she'd been calm. Not untroubled, not carefree, but the mere fact that she could pull herself together at all amazed him.

The calm facade had lasted long enough to get her out of the room. He didn't think she'd expected him to chase her down and she didn't have the strength to project her usual air of insouciant self-reliance. It was like two people lived inside her head, and he wondered which one he'd loved all those years ago.

The old Jillian would have thrown the nearest object at him. She would have ranted and raved, screamed and sworn, scared the hell out of poor little Christine. When he'd first seen her the other day, he'd have sworn the woman he knew hadn't changed one iota, except for acquiring the veneer of sophistication that she'd grown into with adulthood. She'd parried his verbal thrusts skillfully, getting in a few jabs of her own along the way, and he'd sensed the spirit in her.

There was no spirit in the wooden woman who'd walked out of his house tonight.

This new Jillian had damn near cried. He hadn't seen Jillian cry since old Crinkles, the Shar-pei who'd been her childhood companion, died. And that had been when she was fifteen.

Guilt swooped back down from its temporary perch and settled on his shoulders, digging in its claws to roost. He knew the feeling well. He'd felt guilty ever since the day Libby Garrison had knocked on the door of his cheap apartment in Atlanta and told him she was pregnant...less than a year after he'd left Butler County and his bride-to-be.

It didn't help to tell himself he'd been out of his mind, crazy with rage and grief, deliberately trying to erase Jillian from his mind with the willing flesh of other women. What he'd done was wrong. He'd wronged Jillian, and Libby, and most of all, he'd wronged innocent Christine.

His child had deserved a happy, secure home with two parents who loved her and each other...a father who had loved her mother. Dax had never imagined himself a father to any child that wasn't Jillian's, also. A thousand times he'd caught himself comparing Libby to Jillian, wishing for something that would never be.

Yeah, he and guilt had been on pretty intimate terms for a long time.

And now he had a new guilt to live with. Jillian had been more than simply hurt by her unexpected meeting with his child; she'd been decimated. A long time ago, he'd had vengeful dreams of throwing his infidelity in her face. The only thing that had stopped him was uncertainty. She hadn't wanted him any more; why would she care that he'd found other women to replace her?

Tonight, without planning it, he had carried out the satisfying cruelty in that dream. And after seven years, she'd nearly cried tonight...because he'd been unfaithful? But that made no sense given the affair in which he'd caught her with his brother.

He was going to know *why* if he had to stick to her until he was ninety.

The impact hit him again, as he slipped into the cool, clear water for his daily laps, that punishing her had receded to the back of his mind. Experimentally, he probed at the edges of his old anger. Still there. But it didn't consume him as it had since the day he'd planted himself at her side at the funeral. He still wanted to hear her tell him why she'd led him on when it was really Charles she wanted—and he would—but for the first time since he'd walked away from her, he didn't feel driven by the need to make her suffer.

He already had.

No, he didn't want to make her suffer any more. But he needed her to salvage his family's business, his child's heritage. She owed him her cooperation, damn it. And he would do whatever he had to, to ensure that she did exactly that.

She was arranging an adorable autumn outfit custom-made by her friend Deirdre on one of the dolls in her display window when she saw him coming. Through the glass, their eyes met for an instant. Jillian forced herself not to look away, and when his gaze finally dropped, she was gratified.

Until she realized Dax was looking at the cleavage exposed by the open neck of the blouse she wore. She glared at him, but he didn't look up again, so it was a waste of a good evil eye.

Why was he here? Did he plan to rub more salt in the wound? She swallowed. Every time she thought about that evening two weeks ago, the knot in her stomach rose to her throat, almost choking her. *How could he?* How could he have thrown his child in her face?

Then again, why wouldn't he? In his eyes, she had a lot to pay back. Despite his protests, she was sure he'd arranged the "chance" meeting with his daughter.

His daughter. Dax had no reason to know how shattering it had been to come face-to-face with a child of his. *He* wasn't the one whose biological clock had nearly deafened him with its ticking in recent years. She'd been feeling the emptiness of her life more acutely ever since she'd seen the evidence that Dax's life hadn't stopped as hers had when he'd left her.

He reached for the door and the bell above it trilled to announce his coming. She backed out of the display hastily, aware that in her present position the short pink leather skirt she'd worn probably wasn't covering nearly enough of what it was supposed to cover. Ten minutes earlier, she'd been the only one in the store, so it hadn't mattered.

He walked around the display of teddy bears created by a local crafter just as she was tucking her blouse back in more securely.

"Hello, Jillian."

Even the sound of his voice was studded with sharp points that dug into her painfully. She couldn't look at him, so she turned and gathered the unfinished display into a basket she had carried up front, letting the straight bell of her hair swing forward to obscure her face.

"Hello. Is there something I can help you with today?" The hell with cool and polite, she decided. Everybody knew it was better to attack than defend. "Maybe something for that little girl you're so proud of?"

He didn't respond.

Finally, when the cutting response she expected didn't come, she glanced at him.

Dax was studying her soberly, with something that looked suspiciously like compassion replacing the usual onyx glitter in his eyes. "I'd like to talk to you. Here, if that's what you want, or somewhere else after you close."

She shook her head vigorously. "No. You and I have only business concerns, and those can be addressed at board meetings with the other stockholders. We have *nothing* to talk about."

"Have you eaten lunch?"

It was typical Dax, ignoring anything he didn't want to hear.

"No," she said, "And I'm not taking a lunch hour."

"Why not?" For the first time, he surveyed the rest of the store. "I thought your sister worked with you."

She gave him a look that she hoped indicated her assessment of his substandard intelligence quotient. "Do you mean my sister who had a baby four weeks ago and is nursing him around the clock? It's slow in here until about the middle of October, and then things get busy and stay that way until Christmas."

"Don't you have other help?"

"Two part-time girls. And I need to hire more, since Marina won't be working for a while longer." She suddenly realized she was answering his questions as if he were her third-grade teacher, and she turned her back and marched toward the rear of the store. "Goodbye, Dax."

"Do you want to save Piersall Industries?"

The questions stopped her in her tracks. "Of course," she said slowly, wondering where in the world he was going with that question. Obviously he hadn't believed her when she'd told him she hadn't been involved in Charles's business world. She shot him another glare. "I already told you, I don't have anything to do with—"

"I think I can do it but I need your help."

She stared at him for a second, then cupped her left hand around her ear lightly, as if her hearing was faulty. "Say that again."

"I want you to help me save Piersall Industries."

"No. You go right ahead. Hop on your white horse and charge off to the rescue yourself. I have a life of my own to run."

"If you won't help, I don't think I can keep the business from going under." He shook his head.

"You do *not* need me to help with your business empire."

"Yes, I do." He spread his hands on the counter behind which she'd retreated, studying the backs of his big, broad hands. "I want you to marry me. Together, we control enough stock to be sure the company can be managed the way I have in mind."

It *was* possible to be truly speechless. She cast around for words, but not a single phrase floated by. Could he be any more insulting?

"Can I take that as a 'yes'?" He should be laughing at her, but his expression was strangely intense.

"You must have been in an insane asylum all these years," she said, as she finally forced thought to translate to speech. With the return of her voice came outrage. Fury. Damn him! Nobody else in the world could make her lose her temper faster. "I wasn't good enough to marry when you decided your brother and I were having an affair behind your back but now that I own his part of your business, I'm suddenly acceptable?" She picked up a heavy tome of poetry reserved for a customer, feeling the anger flowing through her.

"If you throw that at me, I swear I'll come over this counter after you." He didn't raise his voice a single decibel, but she had the feeling he wasn't kidding. As she slowly, resentfully, lowered the book, he went on. "Are you mad because I left or because I came back with a child?"

"Neither! I'm not mad. To be mad I'd have to care, wouldn't I?" She heard the tremor in her voice and forced strength and venom to mask it. "The only thing I care about is that you jumped to your own conclusions and broke your brother's heart, and you never bothered to admit you could have been wrong. And now he's dead and it's too late."

He winced visibly. When he spoke, his voice was subdued. "How could I have been wrong? I know what I saw. I heard what I heard. Are you claiming I misunderstood something?"

"You, the one who's never made a mistake? Wrong?" It was a sarcastic mutter.

There was a tense silence between them for a moment. Dax eyed her with a thoughtful expression that unnerved her more than she cared to admit. Then the blank regard she couldn't decipher descended, shuttering his thoughts from her. "When would you like to get married? We need to do it soon. There are some things that really can't wait."

"I *don't* like," she said through her teeth. "No."

"Also, I want you in the house because I'm going to need your help and it would be a whole lot easier if you were close by. You'd have your own bedroom," he added, as if that was a magnanimous offer. "And Mrs. Bowley will stay, of course, to keep the house in order. I wouldn't want Christine to be any more upset than she already is."

That stung. He obviously cared for his child. It more than stung, it *burned*. "I'm not interested. Surely there's another woman somewhere who'd be willing to take you on."

A wolfish grin spread across his face. Too late she realized her mistake. "Oh, there are plenty of women who'd be happy to *take me on*, honey-bunch. As I recall, you were one of them once." She made a furious exclamation and he spoke right through it. "But we're talking about something a lot more important than a roll in the hay. Charles left the business in a real bind. If I'm going to prevent bankruptcy, I'm going to need to devote a lot of time to it and I need you to help. In addition, I have my own business concerns to think about."

"Which are?" She concentrated on his words rather than viewing the unwanted images of Dax with another woman that were parading through her brain.

He ignored her. Again. "I'm already negotiating a big account for Piersall to manufacture a new product. I need a hostess. Unfortunately, half of business relationships are social ones. You have the polish—and the knowledge—to be an asset to me."

"I'm flattered." She fanned herself ostentatiously with a hand.

"And you know how to manipulate men into doing just about anything."

She arched an eyebrow. "Oh, my. I've gone from being a hostess to a prostitute in two sentences."

"We'll be married. I'd expect you to act like it. At least in public."

"A snowball in hell would have a better chance."

His mouth tightened, but he didn't explode. "With your education, you can be of considerable help with the financial end of this mess as well. There are some strange things in the books that I'd like your opinion on." He ran a frustrated hand through his crisp black hair. "Even though I have good people in Atlanta, I'm going crazy trying to manage two businesses."

"You don't have far to go." She was pushing him, she knew. But there was no way he was talking her into this insane idea. It would destroy her. "Sounds to me like you need to hire some help."

The glitter came back as his eyes hardened. "That's what I'm trying to do. I want to make some changes in the management structure but I can't do it over the rest of the board's objections unless you back me. Between us, we could get things straightened out enough to hand over a reasonably organized operation to an administrator of our choosing."

"I have a business, in case that's escaped you. I don't need another job."

"You could work with me in the evenings, at the house. You'd never have to go in to the company."

"No wonder you're having trouble managing two businesses—you're deaf." She raised her voice. *"NO!"*

The sound was caught and absorbed by the million and one stuffed toys throughout the shop. She would have loved for it to echo again and again. *No...no...no—*

"Christine needs a mother. You'll do."

She was flabbergasted. She'd thought he couldn't hurt her more. She'd been wrong. "Let her own mother do it," she said acidly. "Or did you run away from her, too?" Pain lanced through her, spearing her heart and she couldn't prevent tears from springing to her eyes. "I have no intention of pretending to show affection for your—"

"Stop right there." His voice cracked with authority and she halted, her anger sidetracked. She'd never heard Dax sound like that when they were younger. Suddenly she was able to see how he'd managed to build a successful business of his own from virtually nothing. "Christine's mother doesn't want her," he said. "She hates my guts and sees my child as a reminder of a marriage she wishes never had occurred."

Jillian knew what it was to be unwanted. But she squashed the empathy that rose. She couldn't be a mother to Dax's child by some other woman. The mere idea was enough to knock the spirit out of her. "Why me?" Hurt dulled her tones and she saw his brows draw together. Furiously, she blinked back the tears. *I will not cry.*

"Why not you? We've practically lived together before. I already know all your annoying habits."

"You don't know me at all," she said bitterly. "I'm not the stupid little girl who hung on every word you uttered anymore."

"I'm well aware that you're not a little girl anymore." He was looking at her mouth and as he spoke, he started around the counter. "And there are *some* things I know for sure." As he reached for her, she backed away, into the little alcove where the staff hung their coats and made drinks.

"I don't want this." Her body screamed, *Liar,* even as her mind recoiled from the horrible reality of being attracted to a man who hated her.

"Too bad. It's the only way I know to shut you up."

She put out her hands to shove him away, but he only grabbed her wrists and held them pinned against the wall on either side of her head as he came up against her, pressing her back against the wall with his big body, and the intimate contact stole her breath away. How could this feel so right, so perfect?

There was a moment of electric stillness, punctuated only by the soft feathering of his breath over her cheek. He leaned into her, flattening her breasts against the solid wall of his chest, so close that she could see the beginnings of the heavy beard he'd probably shaved only a few hours ago. And if he hadn't been holding her hands in place, she might have unthinkingly caressed one lean, tanned cheek to see if the skin over his cheekbones was as taut and firm as it looked. He swallowed, and her eyes followed the movement of his Adam's apple.

"Kiss me," he demanded, and the words saved her from the sensual lethargy that threatened to swamp her.

She knew struggling would be nonproductive so she didn't bother, but turned her face to the side. "Not in this life."

He raised her wrists higher, above her head, and transferred them both to one big hand. Then he took her chin in his hand and forcibly turned her head around. He didn't bother to answer, only set his mouth over hers and began to kiss her.

Their bodies shifted closer, meshed as if they were puzzle pieces perfectly placed. She could feel him, already aroused and growing more so against her, and his mouth devoured hers as if she were a dessert he'd been craving for years.

She hated him; she wasn't going to respond. But her body, long denied the only man who had ever possessed her heart, wasn't about to cooperate, and she could feel her willpower draining away as his tongue flicked along her lip line. After another moment of rigid resistance, her mouth opened beneath his and her body went lax.

As her tongue tentatively met the fierce demand of his, Dax released her wrists and twined his fingers with hers, drawing them down to their sides as their bodies strained against each other. She pulled her hands away from him and slid her palms up his arms in his suit coat, feeling the bulge of muscled biceps beneath the fabric. He'd always kept himself in good shape. It appeared he hadn't changed in that respect.

He cupped one hand around the back of her skull, still holding her lightly for his kissing while the other hand slid surely down over her back to her buttocks, where he filled his hand with her soft flesh and lifted her strongly against him.

She cried out, and he swallowed the sound. For uncounted minutes, they simply explored each other's mouths as he held her pinned against the wall, her body cradling his, his surging against her until the tension in her abdomen was an unbearable taut fist of need and she was meeting his wild thrusts with involuntary circles of her pelvis.

And then he tore his mouth from hers, his hand pressing her face against his shoulder. "Stop," he said in a strangled tone. "Jill, we have to stop."

The words were haunting, a familiar echo from years past.

As if she were surfacing from a great depth, she slowly processed their meaning. Her body still strained toward his, though he took her by the waist and held her away from him. She shook her head, trying to clear it, trying to *think*, and as realization dawned, she stepped away from his hands, turning her back on him and wrapping her arms around herself as if the climate inside the store had taken a turn toward arctic.

Dax blew out a shaking breath. "Holy absolute hell. *That* wasn't part of the plan."

She didn't bother to answer him. She was ashamed. God, she hated herself. And him. This man had believed the worst of her, left her and stayed away until he was forced to come home—and the minute he got near her again, she melted like soft wax to his hot flame.

"I don't want to want you," she said, shuddering.

"That's a futile sentiment," he said. "Bottom line,

honey-bunch, is that we can't keep our hands off each other. Never could, never will."

She whirled to face him, hot anger feeding her shame as she relived her wanton response to his caresses. "Well, here's another bottom line—that's one good reason I won't marry you. Among a host of other, equally valid ones."

He stilled, like a great buck scenting danger. "If you say no, Piersall could go under. It'll cost a lot of people their jobs."

"So you say." She touched her swollen lips to still their trembling. "I have nothing but your word on that." A short, harsh bark of what passed for laughter burst out of her. "And we both know what your promises are worth."

A red tide of color crept up his neck. "Your fault."

"A promise is a promise," she said. "You didn't know anything about what happened between Charles and me. You made an assumption and took off without ever checking out the real truth." Suddenly, she realized what she was saying and she stopped abruptly. She had no intention of trying to vindicate herself in his eyes. Because that would mean she cared about what he thought.

Dax was staring at her like a cat at an irresistibly moving piece of string, his curiosity a palpable presence in the small space where they still stood. She knew he was turning her words over in his mind and the last thing she wanted was more questions.

"Well," she said, as brightly as she could, "As I keep saying, we have nothing to talk about. You can leave now. Want me to make you a flight reservation?"

"I'm not going anywhere," he growled. "Answer me— will you or will you not marry me?"

"Choice *B*," she said. "Not."

His mouth tightened. "All right. I guess that's that." He turned and started for the door. "Any messages for the folks over at Sugar's? Since I'm going that way," he added.

Uneasiness gripped her. "Why are you going next door?"

Dax put his hand on the door knob. "I want to talk to the owner about his lease."

She raced after him and braced her foot against the door. "What are you going to say?"

"That come the end of the month, they'll need to find a new space to lease. Just like you and every other tenant in this building."

"*No!*"

"Then marry me."

"I *can't!*"

"You *won't,*" he corrected, easily opening the door despite her struggles to hold it closed.

Desperate to keep him from going, she blurted, "If I agree to marry you…"

"Not a person in this entire complex will have a thing to worry about."

"You—you *worm.*" She let go of the door and backed up a step, her voice trembling with helpless rage. "This is low. Even for you."

"Yep."

There was a long silence, which she thought resembled nothing so much as an armed standoff. Only he had superior weapons and he knew it.

Her shoulders sagged. "When am I moving in?"

"Tomorrow," he said. "The sooner the better."

She didn't answer; she was too busy trying not to scream. How could she possibly be ready in a day?

Dax must have taken her silence for the possibility of another balk. "Look," he said, "Just do it for six months. If I have things running smoothly by then, you'll be free to leave."

Six months. It was a distant light at the end of a dark tunnel. She nodded slowly, stupidly elated with such a silly little victory. "That's acceptable to me. I have two conditions."

He was suddenly wary, regarding her as he might a cornered snake. "Which are?"

"First, I want a prenuptial agreement that spells out every single part of this despicable deal. Including a promise from you to freeze rents for the next three years."

He thought that over for a moment, then nodded. "All right. What's the second?"

"You can take me to lunch tomorrow and tell me about your daughter."

"My daughter?" He went even more still, and his voice, normally so sure and confident, hesitated, grew as cautious as a first-time skater stepping onto ice.

"If I have to live with this kid, I want to know all about her. *Everything*," she stressed, giving him a level look.

Dax nodded, his eyes searching hers, finding—she hoped—nothing but cool demand. "That's fair."

Four

He took her to the country club, and she wondered how in the world he'd managed to get a membership so fast. Then she remembered that Piersalls had been among the founding members; he probably had a seat with the family name engraved on it.

When the waitress rattled off the specials, Jillian took nasty enjoyment from ordering the lobster entrée—the most expensive item in the house. Although she doubted it would make much of a dent in Dax's pocketbook, if his car and his clothing were an indication of his net worth.

Their drinks arrived, and an awkward silence descended. Dax took a deep breath and she glanced across the table at him, eyebrows raised. He shrugged. "This is...not easy, if you want the truth. I'm not proud of myself."

Good, she thought. She didn't want it to be easy for him. He'd put her through hell and back again; let him squirm a little. "I'd like to hear the truth."

He nodded. "The truth." He picked up his glass and took a hefty swallow of the imported beer he'd ordered. "After you…" He hesitated, and his lips tightened in grim remembrance. Then he went on. "After I left, I wandered for a while. Mother begged me to come home but I didn't want to come back here. I had my trust fund to keep me afloat, and I traveled a little. But after about a month, traveling alone was no fun. I was in Atlanta, so I just stayed. I used the Piersall name to get into a couple of influential doors, and started thinking about how I could get a job with some Atlanta firm. Then an opportunity to buy a small business fell in my lap."

"What business?" He hadn't mentioned anything about how he'd acquired his money, and she'd been dying to know since she'd laid eyes on the Italian leather shoes next to her Magli pumps at the funeral.

He hesitated. "You can't laugh."

"Why would I laugh?" Intrigued despite herself, she leaned forward, trailing her finger over her heart in the shape of a cross. "I promise I won't laugh."

"Travers Coffins."

"*Coffins?*" A bubble of amusement boiled perilously near the edge of her composure and she quickly forced it back, shaking her head. "You make *coffins?*"

He was eyeing her with suspicion. "The baby boomers are aging. It's a growing market and it's only getting bigger."

She nodded wisely, seriously. She hoped. "Makes sense to me."

"You *are* laughing," he accused. "This is exactly why I didn't tell you before."

"I'm sorry." She put one hand over her mouth and motioned him to proceed. "I just wasn't expecting *that.*"

"Neither was I," he said dryly. "But as I said, it was a great opportunity. So I used some of my trust to buy it."

He took another drink, and she did the same, figuring a little Dutch courage couldn't hurt.

"I hired a couple of people right away, and added others later. The first executive assistant was a girl—woman—named Olivia Garrison. Libby. She was young, like me, fresh out of college with a brand-new degree in finance, and she was really sharp."

A stab of envy shot through her. Dax had thought her many things in their long association, but she doubted he'd ever praised *her* intelligence to anyone.

"I had an affair with her," he said. His eyes had gone hard and cold and he watched her like a hawk.

Carefully, she kept her expression neutral. His affairs meant nothing to her. *And maybe if you tell yourself that enough, you'll even begin to believe it.*

"One night, after a business dinner with some suppliers, I left her standing in front of the restaurant while I went and got the car. When I pulled around front, she was standing in profile, with her face turned away from me—and for a minute, I saw you." He drummed his fingers on the table and his face was set as he went on. "It hit me then, that I'd picked her because she reminded me of you. Subconsciously, maybe I figured she looked enough like you that I could replace you with her in my damned dreams."

She made an instinctive sound of denial. Why had she asked about his stupid kid anyway? She should have known he would turn it into one more opportunity to rub her nose in the failure of their engagement, which he perceived to be her fault. But Dax was still speaking and the words penetrated her mind despite her best efforts to ignore them.

"Our...fling didn't last long, and it wasn't the only one. Unfortunately, the God of Birth Control was on vacation, and that February, she told me she was pregnant."

February. She took deep breaths, trying to still the buzzing in her head. *He'd gotten another woman pregnant less than a year after he'd left her.* If she'd had any doubt about how little she'd really meant to him, there was none left now. She held up her hand, and her voice was a whisper. "Stop."

"No way. You wanted to hear it. You can tough it out." When she tried to rise, Dax caught her hands and held her in her seat. "Christine was born October third. Libby and I got married a few months before her birth."

That was a perfect entry for another cutting comment. But for the life of her, she couldn't think of one. Misery washed over her in great waves and now she did stop listening, staring at the big hands imprisoning hers.

They were strong and blunt, the backs covered with silky black hair that she knew was repeated in other places all over his body. Those hands had touched her with love once, long ago when she'd had dreams of being the love of his life, of being the mother of his children.

But instead, he'd found someone else.

As she stared at his hands, they seemed to recede down a long tunnel, like the inside of a kaleidoscope, only the black around the edges impinged upon the color more and more, squeezing the perfect circle of her vision into a teeny dot of color—

"Jillian!" Dimly, she realized Dax was holding her. She wanted to struggle away but lethargy kept her limbs from bothering to respond to her sluggish brain. He put a hand at the back of her neck and held her head down between her knees. "Take deep breaths."

Vision began to return and she cautiously raised her head. People were staring at them around the dining room, but at a glance from Dax, they quickly looked away again.

"Here. Take a drink. You still look white enough to faint." He held a glass of water to her lips, and she sipped obediently. Then she realized she was in his lap.

"I don't faint," she said irritably, trying to get away

from the contact. Beneath her bottom, his thighs were hard, his body warm, his arm firm and muscled against her back, and if she didn't loathe him so much, she happily could have nestled in for a decade or two. They tussled for a minute, and he finally set her in her own seat again—probably because she was attracting attention with all her flopping around.

"I don't faint," she said again.

"Okay, you don't faint." Dax smiled, and there was a touch too much warmth and gentleness in it. She didn't want him warm and gentle, damn it. He was much easier to hate when he was being overbearing and unfriendly.

"It was the alcohol on an empty stomach, that's all. Give me those crackers," she demanded, indicating the generous plate of cheese and crackers they'd ignored until now.

As he handed her the plate, he said quietly, "If it makes you feel any better, the marriage was a disaster from the first day. It took Libby about five minutes to figure out that she was a substitute for you."

She'd expected bitterness, and was caught off-guard by the weary resignation in his tone. "If you hated me so much why did you tell her about me?"

He raised his gaze to her puzzled one, and now there was bitterness, as well as cynical self-mockery in the look. "I didn't," he said flatly. "But calling your name in the middle of the night—and other times—kind of tipped her off."

It wasn't fair. There should be some satisfaction in knowing that he'd been as miserable as she. But images of Dax with another woman rose to taunt her and she found herself fighting back the lump rising in her throat. To combat it, she summoned up her attack strategies.

"Let me guess," she said, raising a brow mockingly. "She left you before you could explain what *really* happened."

There was a silence as he absorbed the dig. But all he said was, "No. She didn't leave me. It took about four years for me to decide that all we were doing was ruining Christine's life with our constant fighting. I moved out and asked for a divorce." His mouth twisted. "Libby found somebody to replace me fast enough. The problem is that he doesn't want another man's kid around. And Libby only sees Christine as a reminder of a lousy time in her life."

"So she's with you for, what, vacation? Visitation?" She forced out the words, ignoring the ache in her throat. She didn't want to like Dax's child, didn't want to care about her. But this tragic story aroused every ounce of maternal instinct she possessed. How could anyone fail to love their own child, no matter what the circumstances?

After he'd left, after she'd finally realized he was never coming back, she'd cried nightly for months. God, she'd wanted children of her own, children of *his,* so badly....

Dax shook his head, and his expression darkened. "I was awarded full custody of Christine a year ago. Libby hasn't called her, hasn't been to see her since. From now on, all my little girl has is me. And you," he added. "Since you're her stepmother."

"Hardly." Stepmother. It was getting hard to breathe.

"You will be in a few days." His expression grew grim. "And I'd appreciate it if you could try not to traumatize her further when you move in."

Her hand shook as she reached for her water, and droplets splashed across the white table cloth. "I can't do this."

"You've already agreed to it."

"You mean, 'been coerced into.'" She could hardly contain her distress.

Dax's eyes were cool. He leaned forward and mopped at the spill without taking his gaze from her. "It's your own fault."

"It is *not* my fault," she whispered over the ache in her

throat. "*I never left you.* I wasn't cheating on you with your brother—I *loved* you, Dax." She looked away from his intense, uncomprehending gaze, unable to resist protesting her innocence one last time. "I trusted you, apparently a whole lot more than you trusted me."

He crossed his arms and leaned back, eyeing her with distant interest. "I guess now you want to tell me your version of how you and Charles wound up trading 'I love yous' in bed together while you were wearing my ring."

She put down the cracker she had been nibbling, all interest in food gone. He would never believe a word she said, and she should know better than to dream for one little minute of setting the record straight between them. "You know what? This was a really lousy idea. Let's pretend we just finished our coffee and dessert and get out of here."

"Don't you want your lobster?"

"No." She rose. "I'm leaving."

He stood and signaled for the check, assisting her to her feet and holding her elbow when she would have bolted out of the room ahead of him.

"Someday," he said, looking down at her as he helped her into his BMW, one hand on the door frame and the other braced against the roof. "Someday it *will* be your turn to talk. And I've already started making my list of questions."

As he rounded the back of the car, Jillian looked off across the parking lot, wishing she could snap her fingers and be home, and end this miserable afternoon. Movement caught her eye, and she recognized Roger Wingerd escorting a woman into the club. At the same moment, he saw her. A distinctly wary expression crossed his features, but he altered his course and came toward the car. Well, she couldn't blame him, poor man, after the way Dax had acted last time they'd met.

"Hello, Roger," she said through her open window.

"Hello, Jillian," he said. He bent to nod through the window at Dax. "Mr. Piersall."

Dax nodded. "Wingerd. I'll be seeing you at the board meeting next Tuesday."

"Ah, yes." Roger nodded. "Will you be assuming an active role in the company? Charles was in accord with the rest of the board—"

"I've read the reports," Dax interrupted. "And frankly, I doubt that I'll be as easy to get along with as Charles apparently was. I'm not impressed with the way the company has been handled."

Roger's eyebrows rose, but his tone was mild. "The rest of the stockholders haven't been unhappy, but I'm sure they'll be glad to entertain your ideas."

"Good." Dax turned the key and the Beamer's engine roared to life with a muted growl. "I'll be happy to offer them." And without waiting for a reply, he reversed and began to drive out of the parking lot.

"You know," Jillian said, "There's an old saying that you can catch more flies with sugar than you can with...other substances. It couldn't hurt to at least *pretend* to be courteous to your employees."

Dax shrugged. "Wingerd may not be an employee for long. I intend to make some major changes in the company's structure."

She was horrified. "But you can't just barge in there and start axing people! Roger's been a loyal employee. The rest of the board will never agree."

"Maybe not. But it doesn't really matter what they think. With the majority vote, I intend to move the company in the direction I've decided we need to go."

"So you're just going to march in there and start issuing orders? Getting rid of faithful employees?" And why did he assume their marriage would give him her votes automatically?

"I'm not going to fire employees wholesale. I don't particularly enjoy the thought. But if we don't streamline and tighten a little, *everyone* who's employed there will be out of work. Is that what you want? Piersall was started by my grandfather, and I'd like to hand it down to Christine someday. I have no intention of letting the current situation get any worse."

She didn't answer him. But the glimmer of an idea had blossomed in her mind. Tuesday's board meeting might be more interesting than even Dax planned.

The rest of the week passed far too quickly for Jillian's peace of mind.

Dax arranged a brief civil ceremony at the courthouse on Friday morning. The witnesses would be two people who were paid for their services, because she'd flatly refused to have anyone she knew attend.

On Thursday, they met at his lawyer's office to sign the prenuptial contract she'd requested. It was short and succinct, and her lawyer had reviewed it and made a few pertinent changes, much to Dax's annoyance. Each of them would retain any assets they brought to the marriage; if she stayed a minimum of six months, Dax would fulfill the terms of the rental lease of her store location as he'd indicated previously.

They met in the courthouse hallway the next morning. The only concession she'd made for the occasion was to pull an elegant ivory silk suit from her closet that morning. She'd insisted on driving herself in from the store. She had a lunch date with her closest friends and she saw no reason to pretend this was anything more than a business arrangement. Keeping everything as superficial as she possibly could was the only way she would get through this horrible farce. Not that she'd ever let Dax know that.

"Don't you want your sister or a friend to be here?" Dax asked her. "We still have time to call them."

"What for?" she said as they walked toward the judge's chambers. "It isn't as if this is a real wedding." She shuddered, remembering the weddings of her sister and both of her best friends in recent years. Those ceremonies had been filled with so much love and tenderness that she'd nearly ruined her image by crying at each one of them. This, she was determined, would be as unmemorable as she could possibly make it, as far from the dreams and expectations she'd once had as the sun was from the moon.

Dax looked down at her. "It *is* a real wedding," he said in a cool, remote voice. "It will be as binding as anything you've ever done in your life, honey-bunch, and I expect you to remember it."

"Or what?" she asked flippantly. "The last time you got mad at me you picked up all your toys and moved out of town. Can I get that lucky again?"

Rage kindled in his eyes. "I'm older and wiser now," he said through his teeth as the door to the judge's chambers opened and the couple before them entered. "If I catch you being unfaithful this time, you'll wish you'd never been born."

The promising menace in his voice subdued the sharp response she'd been about to make, and once again, she realized how little she knew about the man he'd become. And she didn't care, she told herself firmly. She only had to endure this for six months, let Dax get his precious family business straightened out, and then she'd be gone from his life as fast and finally as he'd left hers seven years ago.

It was their turn all too quickly, and before she knew it, she was standing before the judge exchanging vows with Dax. It was passionless and utterly forgettable, and she was glad. This wasn't a marriage in her eyes and this stupid ceremony certainly wasn't anything to remember. It might legally bind her to Dax but this way she could pretend she was living a bad dream for the next few months.

Near the end of the short ceremony, though, she was jolted into full alertness when Dax produced two sets of rings from his pocket at the judge's request.

Hastily, she put both hands behind her back. "I don't need a ring."

"Oh, yes, you do." Dax took her arm and tugged, his fingers digging into her soft flesh until she released her clasped hands and let him drag her left hand forward. He slipped a delicate, beautifully designed diamond with an interlocking wedding band onto her finger and then turned his hand in hers, practically forcing her to slip the ring he handed her onto his finger.

Without making a scene in front of the judge, she could hardly refuse, though she was tempted. She wouldn't, however, look at him or their hands as the judge concluded the words that sealed her fate. Dax didn't attempt to kiss her, which, in her opinion, showed intelligence on his part. When she signed the license, her hand shook as she wrote her name.

"I'm keeping my name," she said as she handed him the pen.

"We'll discuss it later."

"There's nothing to discuss," she said in a dismissive tone.

Dax didn't respond, but she cast him a wary glance. He wasn't usually so easy to defy, and his silence made her wonder what he was up to.

They emerged from the courthouse and she blinked in the hot sun of the autumn day. She fumbled in her purse for her sunglasses, sighing in relief when she'd shoved them onto her nose. Dax didn't appear to mind the sudden change in light at all. He took her by the elbow again as they crossed the street to the parking lot where their cars waited, something she'd noticed he did with annoying regularity, and she pulled free.

"Hands off. This ring doesn't give you any more privileges than you had before."

He slanted her a dark, knowing smile. "My touch bothers you that much?"

"Your touch is so insignificant as to be unnoticed in my life." Even though every cell in her body was aware of him pacing along beside her.

"Unnoticed?"

"Completely."

"Well, then, I guess you wouldn't notice this, either." She'd forgotten that Dax hated to lose an argument even more than she did, but the knowledge came crashing back as his hand seized her elbow again. This time, though, it wasn't a simple, courteous gesture.

This time, he swung her around to face him, sliding an arm around her waist before she even registered his intent. His face loomed in her vision as it neared hers, and she gasped as he used pressure at the small of her back to pull her solidly against him right there in the middle of the parking lot. The gasp died half-issued, though, as he took her mouth in an intimate, searing kiss that demanded a response.

She went rigid with denial. *No!* She didn't want this, didn't want him, didn't *want* to want him. But even as that streaked through her mind, a much more primitive response took over.

Her body became someone else's when he touched her. It seemed to belong to some willing, wanton woman who writhed beneath his hands, seeking a better fit for the hard strength of his body against hers, opening her mouth willingly for his invasion and welcoming the bold strokes of his tongue with her own. This other woman's breasts tingled with arousal where they were dragged over the unyielding planes of his chest, and her loins throbbed with inviting pleas for fulfillment.

When he raised his head, she could do nothing but cling to him, limp and unresisting. He still held her to him as his penetrating gaze swept over her face. Dimly, she realized that Dax was angry, but that he'd retained control while pushing her beyond the edges of her own.

But he was breathing as harshly as she. Whatever punishment he'd intended this to be had gotten out of his control as well.

"I don't love you," he said, and the words sliced straight through a heart she thought he'd already damaged beyond repair years ago. "But I still want you, and you want me, regardless of what you say to the contrary. Tonight we'll do something about it."

"No," she said in a shaking voice, pushing belatedly at his chest. "If you come near me tonight, I swear I'll leave town. I don't care what you do, you're not forcing me to sleep with you."

"Oh, I wouldn't have to force you," he said in a voice silky with satisfaction. "You and I both know there'd be no force involved."

"Maybe not." She pushed her sunglasses to the top of her head. Her voice was regaining steadiness, and she fixed eyes dulled with resignation on his. "But it would still be force because it's not what I want. If you can live with that, then fine."

The muscles in the arms still holding her went taut for a moment, and a muscle in his lean cheek throbbed. Then he released her with a short bark of frustrated laughter. "You sure do know how to take the fun out of a wedding day, honey-bunch."

And as she watched him walk away, she touched a finger

to lips that still throbbed from his kisses. Living in the same house with him was going to be the hardest thing she'd ever done in her life.

Because no matter how loud or long she protested to the world, her heart still yearned for him. She hated him and she loved him, and she wasn't sure she could resist him again if he was determined to have her.

She was a little late arriving at the café where she'd agreed to meet her friends for lunch because she'd sat in her car calming herself down for ten minutes after Dax had finally left. And then it had occurred to her that he'd been wearing most of her lipstick when he left, so she pulled out her purse and systematically repaired her makeup. The last thing she needed was for Frannie and Dee to grill her about her relationship with Dax. This was going to be hard enough to explain as it was.

The temptation not to mention her marriage to either her friends or her sister was strong. But the holidays were coming, and she didn't see how she was going to get around it. If it were only her and Dax it would be different. But there was Christine to think about. A child required holiday preparations and events and she would have too much awkward maneuvering to do if she hid the fact of this marriage from everyone.

For the first time, she allowed herself to really remember the child with whom she'd been confronted that evening at Dax's home. According to what he had told her since, the little girl would be six now...seven next month.

She'd been tall for her age. Blond, slender, with wide blue eyes.

I figured she looked enough like you that I could replace you with her in my damned dreams.

He'd certainly done a good job of trying. Except for the set of the little girl's jaw, which marked her as Dax's issue, she could have been Jillian's. It gave her little satisfaction to know that she'd ruined his effort without even knowing it.

Men were such idiots. She hadn't married, had never had children because she'd known, instinctively, that there could never be another Dax in her life, and she hadn't been willing to settle for less. She'd mourned her lack of children, but had never been able to bring herself to cold-bloodedly marry a man she didn't love simply to fulfill her desire for a family.

He, on the other hand....

She shook back her hair and pulled open the café's heavy glass door. She was *not* going to let him ruin the rest of her day. It would be bad enough when he found out she had no intention of sleeping at his home tonight, or any night until she moved in her furniture. Right now, she was going to try to relax and explain this to her friends.

Frannie Ferris and Dee Sullivan, her two closest friends, were seated already, and they waved at her across the crowded little room. She wound her way through the maze of tables, embracing each of them as they rose to greet her.

"Hello, hello. Let me see." She paused and peered at both of their faces with exaggerated attention. "Everybody must be sleeping through the night. I don't see any dark circles under your eyes."

As they all settled at the table, Frannie gave a quiet chuckle. "Yes, at long last, everyone in the Ferris household is sleeping the whole night through. We were so spoiled with Alexa and Ian that Brittany was a double shock, the little stinker."

Jillian smiled as she picked up the drink they'd ordered for her. Frannie's youngest child would be a year old in December and had been the fussiest infant in recorded history. Once they'd accepted the fact that Brittany simply seemed to need to scream for a few hours a day, Frannie and her husband Jack had relaxed and quit worrying that something was wrong.

"Things are very good at our house," Dee confessed, laughing when Frannie stuck out her tongue. Dee's new daughter Maureen was only four months old and already she was sleeping soundly. "Lee loves first grade and Tommy's just as thrilled with kindergarten. He even says he's happy having time at home with Ronan and me without Lee."

"That's good to hear," Jillian said. She knew Deirdre had been worried about how her younger son was going to cope with his brother's absence during his first year of all-day school. Then she sat forward. "I have some big news. Any guesses?"

Frannie eyed her speculatively. "How big?"

"*Very* big."

Both women looked intrigued.

"You're buying a new business." Frannie sat back with a satisfied air.

"Wro-o-ong." She drew out the word like a gong.

"Going on another cruise?"

"That's not big news," Dee objected as Jillian shook her head. "You're selling your condo?" The smallest woman lifted a hand to indicate she was mystified.

"No, but I'm renting it out."

"What?" Frannie looked puzzled. "Why would you do that? Where are you moving?"

Jillian smiled into the drink she lifted to her lips. She took a deep breath and prepared to act with all the skill she possessed "It's a long story. But I guess it starts with...this." She brought up her left hand and waggled her ring finger under her friends' noses, giving her best imitation of a woman thrilled to be showing off her new gift.

Both women's mouths dropped open.

"Those are diamonds!" Dee exclaimed.

"No!" Jillian was glad she could find something to be amused about. She wanted to avoid sympathy at all costs.

"There's a wedding band as well as a diamond!" Frannie said. "Do you have someone you'd like us to meet?" Her soft brown eyes sparkled with interest.

"I do." She held up a warning finger. "But it's not exactly the kind of story you're expecting to hear."

"Well, it's a love story," Dee said, sighing happily. "That's all I care about."

"No, it's not."

"What?" Dee sat up straight in her chair. "Tell, Jill. You're not making any sense."

"Okay." Jillian say back again, toying with the ring. "I got married this morning." She ignored her friends' startled exclamations and went on. "His name is Dax Piersall and we grew up together. He's Charles's older brother."

"Your friend who was killed," Frannie said softly.

"Right." Jillian gazed at the ring. "Charles left me his chunk of the company. Dax and I are making a temporary business merger because there seem to be some problems with company management and we need to straighten things out."

"You got *temporarily* married to this guy?" Frannie looked stunned. "I don't understand. Surely you two could have worked together without a marriage."

"No," Jillian said. "Trust me. It's better this way." She refused to bare the ugly details of either her past with Dax or the deal he'd forced upon her. If she had to eat humiliation, she'd do it privately.

"How long will you be married?" Dee asked. Her heart-shaped face was drawn into a mask of bewildered concern. "And where will you be living?"

"I'm moving into Dax's home on the other side of Butler County. We agreed on six months." She twisted the ring on her finger, deliberately attempting to lighten the atmosphere. "You know, he didn't tell me if I could keep the rings when this is all said and done. Guess I'll have to work on that one."

"You're hiding something," Frannie accused. "What are you not telling us?"

"Just details, lots of boring details. It's really a pretty simple deal. Oh, and Dax has a daughter, so I'm going to become a stepmama."

"Oh, boy, the plot thickens. How old is his daughter?" asked Dee.

"Just a little older than Lee, actually. I imagine she's in first grade as well."

"Where were you married?"

Jillian quickly saw where Frannie was going with her train of thought. Frannie ran a business designing wedding gowns; her feelings were going to be bruised that Jillian hadn't let her design a gown for her. "We went down to the courthouse about two hours ago," she said hastily. "I wore this. Really, it was no big deal. We didn't even have any witnesses."

"Just like a business merger," Dee said softly.

"Exactly." Jillian raised her glass. "In six months, I'll be a free woman again. And hopefully, a wealthier one, as well." She leaned forward and patted Frannie's hand. "I promise, if I ever get married and *mean it,* you can have a free hand in the gown department. Anything you like."

Frannie smiled wryly. "Somehow, I find that promise has a hollow ring, coming from a woman who's a more committed bachelor than most single men I know."

"I'll consider that a compliment." She smiled and raised her glass. "Shall we drink to my temporary matrimonial state?"

The other women dutifully raised their glasses in a celebratory toast, but as the waitress rushed by to take their lunch orders, she had the uncomfortable feeling that neither of her friends was satisfied with the illusion she'd created.

Five

Dax stood looking out the window in the study that faced the circular driveway fronting the house. He'd believe she was really coming when he saw her.

When she told him she needed time to pack before she moved in, Dax could tell from her combative tone that Jillian expected him to object. And because he knew that was what she expected, he even gave her a week, extracting her promise to move in on Saturday. That was plenty of time, he figured, for her to get organized and get her pretty little butt into his house, where it belonged now that she had his ring on her finger.

She'd refused to give up her condo, though. She'd left almost everything there, saying she would lease it for six months...an unsubtle reminder of that stupid time limit he'd blurted out when he'd thought she was going to refuse every coercion he'd thrown at her. He'd been forced to use the threat of losing her business, and those of her friends, to get her to agree at all, and it stuck in his throat that she'd turned him into such an ogre.

Didn't she know him well enough to know that he'd never really do any such thing?

Her ongoing enmity was beginning to get to him. Since the day she'd met Chris—the day he'd seen her flashy facade crack and the real woman who suffered behind it—he had thought less and less of how many ways he could wring her neck.

And after the way she'd overreacted again in the restaurant, he *knew* she was hurting. He just didn't know why. Yet.

But right now, as they had been since he'd seen her again, his thoughts now were concerned with the gorgeous physical package she presented. He was tired of fighting the attraction, tired of pretending he didn't want to touch, taste, feel every inch of her. He didn't have to love her, or even like her, to want her. If "want" was the right word for the rushing, surging river of sexual desire that flooded his system every time he so much as thought about her. Or touched her. And when she was actually *with* him, it would be so much better…no, he wasn't fighting it anymore.

He was going to have her.

Oh, he knew she'd agreed to this marriage with the expectation that she'd have a separate room from his. And that was fine with him.

They could romp in her bed as easily as they could in his.

Three vans, one emblazoned with a logo that read Brooks Bridals, turned up the circular drive and pulled to a stop in front of the door. Hastily, he moved away from the study window and parked himself at his desk, just in case she might think, mistakenly, that he'd been watching for her.

He heard the slamming of doors, and the chatter of women's voices underlaid with deep masculine tones, and he bent his head over the printouts before him. The study door was open, though, and the noise spilled into the house as Jillian's moving forces trooped in.

He caught a flash of Jillian, in something shocking pink and *skimpy,* and then he heard her feet on the stairs. "This way, fellas," she called, leading them to the room he'd showed her a few days ago.

A big blond man staggered past under a load of clothes-hangered garments. "Explain to me again why *I* have to do this? She's *your* friend."

Brown hair and lemon shorts that displayed legs he'd like to get a better look at followed the giant. "Yeah? Well, just remember—she showed you mercy when you didn't deserve any a few years ago. If she hadn't, you wouldn't have lived long enough to see me again!" Both people laughed.

Two more men came by, carrying suitcases under arms, in fingers, over shoulders. Then two more. Jillian flashed by again. "Where are those tabloid photographers when you need them?" she asked the empty air. "I can see it now. Best-selling Suspense Novelist's Marriage Wrecked By Stunning Blonde."

"How about Mediocre Author Killed By Vengeful Wife," said a short, dark-haired and incredibly nicely stacked woman as they passed.

Both women cackled with glee and a man out of his sight behind them said, "Hey. I take exception to that."

Wondering just what in hell they were talking about, and who exactly was in this moving team, he got up and went to the door.

"Here." Jillian dragged an enormous suitcase in and thrust it at him. "You take that up and I'll get another load."

He might have refused, but he was too curious now, so he hefted the bag and mounted the stairs. Four men passed him on the landing, giving him curious looks and a wide berth. They were all big, thick-necked and tanned. And young.

It figured.

Manhandling the heavy case through the doorway, he dropped it—hard—beside a stack of others on the floor. As he stepped back, he was aware of the examination going on.

Of him.

"Hey." The blond man who offered his hand was even bigger up close, and he didn't relish the thought of putting his palm against that meaty ham. But a guy had to do what a guy had to do. He went in gripping hard and quickly squeezed as powerfully as he could, then released the hand and stepped back before the man's grip tightened.

Victory! He still had all his fingers. "Hello," he said. "I'm Dax Piersall. Jillian's husband," he added, just in case there was any doubt.

"Jack Ferris." The other man looked him over as if he was checking for fleas. "This is my wife, Frannie."

"Hello." He shook Frannie Ferris's hand far more gently than he had her husband's. She owned the legs he'd seen, and close up, she was quietly beautiful with intense brown eyes and light brown hair streaked by the summer sun. "Did I hear you say a few minutes ago that Jillian is your friend?"

Frannie nodded, giving him a small, measuring smile, and he realized these people thought of themselves as Jillian's protectors. The very idea of Jillian needing anyone's protection tickled his funny bone and he returned the smile widely. Then the shattered look he'd put on her face twice in the recent past came into his head, and his smile faded.

He turned to the second couple, holding out a hand. "I'm Dax. More friends of Jillian's?"

The man stepped forward and shook his hand. He

seemed far more civilized than Jack Ferris, and his grip was firm, brief and businesslike. "Ronan Sullivan. 'Friend' is a strong word. Jillian only tolerates me. My wife, Deirdre, is the one who claims friendship." He reached back for his wife's hand and she came forward.

"It's nice to meet you, Dax." She was a stunner with a sultry, husky voice and the greenest eyes he'd ever seen. She was also sweetly shy, clinging to her husband's hand. Add the truly awesome figure neatly tucked into her shorts and shirt, and the black waist-length curls she had tried to confine with a headband, and he could see why Sullivan wasn't letting go of that hand.

And then Jillian reentered the room and he had no trouble erasing all other thoughts from his mind. She was wearing what looked like an exercise bra and skin-tight bike shorts in the eye-popping pink he'd seen, with chunky socks and serious sneakers that looked well broken in. He hadn't seen her so briefly dressed before, and the impact of her slim, softly rounded shape was so forceful that he felt as if he'd staggered backward. And mentally, he had.

She was muscled in all the right places. Firm arms, taut thighs, not an extra ounce on her bare, tanned midriff. Ronan said, "Jill, I want to thank you for that outfit. And I mean that sincerely."

Jack started to chuckle.

Jillian grinned. "I dug it out just for you, dear."

Dax had to restrain the impulse to plant his fist squarely in the middle of the dark-haired man's grinning face.

"Did you tell him?" she asked Ronan.

"Tell him what?"

Jillian gave a disgusted snort. "I know you're not modest so it must be general orneriness." Turning to Dax, she said, "Ronan is R. A. Sullivan."

R. A. Sullivan! He recognized the novelist's name immediately. "You're kidding," he said. "I read your books all the time. I have them all in hardback."

"More pennies in his pocket," said Jack. "Me, I wait and buy 'em when they come out in paperback."

Ronan gave the big man a dry look. "Cheap creep."

Then Jillian faced him again, and he saw a surprising uncertainty in her eyes. "Has everyone else been introduced?"

He nodded. "Every single one of us. Now, how much more stuff do you have crammed into those vans?"

Jack grimaced. "You don't want to know. But if we wait long enough, maybe the other guys will bring it all up for us."

"They're members of Jack's lacrosse team," Frannie informed Dax. "Impressed into service by the coach."

He looked at Jillian again. "Is there more stuff at the condo you want to get?"

She shook her head. The uncertainty had faded and the mantle of confidence she usually wore so easily was back. "Nope. Six months and then I'm outta here, buddy."

A silence descended on the room. It felt like everyone—except Jillian, who was openly smirking—was holding their breath, waiting for his reaction.

He would have dragged her out of the room for a private confrontation, except that he was afraid that if he put his hands on all that bare skin, he'd be shooting himself in the foot.

Instead, he put his hands in his pockets and shrugged, turning to her friends. "She gets combative when she feels threatened, and right now I'm making her nervous as hell."

Jack hooted and Ronan gave a long whistle, but his words had the predictable effect on Jillian. He could practically see the fur rising. In another minute she'd be hissing and spitting. Just as she opened her mouth—to blast him, no doubt—he said, "Go ahead and call me names, honey-bunch. You can make it up to me later...when we're alone."

If those blue eyes could shoot bullets, he'd be bleeding to death at her feet. Jillian paused, almost gave in to the urge to say something, then sniffed and stomped out of the room.

"Hey, *honey-bunch,* wait for me." Jack headed after her with Ronan on his heels. "You have to tell the guys where you want them to set that little table."

There was a short, uncomfortable silence behind the trio's departure.

Dax was still patting himself on the back for winning that skirmish when Deirdre Sullivan approached. She looked as nervous as he'd claimed Jillian was, but her little pointed chin was up and her eyes were determined.

"Jillian told us this was a business deal."

He nodded. "That's one way to explain it."

"I'd like to hear *your* way to explain it." She crossed her arms.

Dax was surprised. Who'd have ever thought this one would be Jillian's champion? Mildly, he said, "I think that's better left between my wife and me."

"When Jillian told us, this wedding idea sounded like a simple business maneuver," Frannie murmured, moving up behind her friend. "But it doesn't seem simple now that I've seen you two together."

He gave her a bland look. "We've known each other most of our lives."

"Jill's not as tough as she acts," Deirdre informed him. "I don't know why you've come back or why she's really coming to live with you, but please, please don't hurt her."

"Any more," Frannie added.

Dax raised his eyebrows, wondering just what in hell Jillian had told her friends about him. "Whoa. Who says I did?"

Frannie didn't smile. "Nobody *said* anything. But if it wasn't you, then someone else slammed her down and kicked her a few dozen times in the past. Can you tell me it *wasn't* you?"

"Look," he said, beginning to feel a little like a porpoise in the midst of a pod of Orcas, "Jillian and I have a lot of history together, and some things to iron out. I'm not—" He stopped abruptly. He could not stand here and lie to these two women. He *had* come back to hurt her. And he'd succeeded. But the success had created more questions than it had quelled.

"I have hurt her," he said quietly, rubbing the back of his neck. "And I'm not sure I won't again. But I won't hurt her on purpose." He lifted his hands. "That's the best I can do."

"I'd appreciate it if you wouldn't embarrass me in front of my friends." Jillian stood in the doorway, spoiling for a fight. She'd been here for twenty-four hours and hadn't spoken to Dax since their verbal battle in front of Frannie, Dee and their husbands.

Dax was sitting comfortably in a chair in the homey family room Charles had preferred to the more formal areas of the house, watching a baseball game on the sports channel. He glanced up at her words. "Then don't bait me."

She made a pretense of looking at her watch, saw that Christine was playing in the room and decided to abandon the attack. "What do you want for dinner tonight? Am I expected to make the meals when Mrs. Bowley is off?"

Dax blew out a huge, exaggerated sigh. "Of course not. You can cook if you'd like, or I will, but Mrs. Bowley usually leaves us a casserole."

Christine was sitting on the floor with a scattering of dolls and clothing surrounding her. Her head had jerked up at Jillian's entrance and her eyes had followed the conversation as if she were watching a tennis match. Now she said, "Oh, Daddy, it's tuna-noodle. Yuck." She climbed into Dax's lap and looked into his face. "Can we order pizza?"

Dax laughed at her, walking his fingers up her spine until she wriggled away, squealing. "Nope. Tuna casserole's fine with me."

"Well, it's not fine with me. I can't stand tuna casserole." Jillian turned to leave the room. She felt small and mean, being jealous of a child, but she couldn't bear to watch the open adoration in Christine's eyes as she looked at her father, nor his tender affection. "I'm going to see what else I could make for tonight's meal. I'll freeze the tuna. Some day when Christine and I are out, you can eat it alone," she informed him.

She went into the big kitchen and yanked open doors, drawers and closets in search of possibilities for meal-making. A bag of tomatoes in the refrigerator had her thinking spaghetti, so she put a pot of water on to boil and cored the tomatoes while she waited.

She was assembling herbs and getting ready to chop a bell pepper when Christine came through the swinging door. The little girl gave her one swift glance and then made herself as small as possible in a far corner. Which was fine with Jillian.

She chopped up the pepper, as well as an onion, which she held under the running tap as much as possible so her eyes wouldn't tear. As she prepared to drop the tomatoes into the now-boiling pot of water, Christine came to the counter and peered over the edge at the preparations. "Whatcha makin'?"

"Spaghetti sauce." Plop, plop, plop. The tomatoes went in, came out and immediately she immersed them in a pan of ice water so the skins would slip off neatly.

"I like spaghetti sauce," Christine informed her.

It wasn't a question, so Jillian didn't answer. Though she knew it was irrational to blame this child for her father's sins, it was hard not to resent her. The old, familiar ache tugged at her.

"Daddy told me you're going to be my stepmother now." Christine peeped through her lashes to gauge the effect of her words.

"I guess I am," Jillian said steadily.

"Do I call you stepmother?"

Jillian had to laugh. "No, that reminds me too much of Snow White. You can call me Jill if you like. That's what my friends call me."

Christine was silent for a moment, but her small hands twisted her doll's curls into painful-looking knots. "I don't have any friends," she said.

She really did not want to like this child, did *not* want to care, but her soft heart couldn't resist the loneliness in the little voice. She and loneliness were far too well acquainted for her to wish its presence on Christine. Laying down her knife, she turned and knelt in front of the girl.

Christine immediately shrank back, clearly startled, but Jillian pretended she hadn't noticed. "I'm going to take you to visit your new school on Monday. I bet that you'll make some friends there." She smiled, wanting the wariness to fade from those wide eyes. "Did Daddy tell you about my family?"

Christine shook her head. The doll with the abused hair was tightly clutched to her chest now.

"You have some cousins now, and an aunt and uncle." Then she stopped. Was it wrong to let the child get to know her family? Had Dax told Christine that Jillian was only going to be here six months? Somehow, she doubted it.

But Christine's eyes were wide and interested now. "Cousins?"

"Um-hmm." Jillian rose and picked up her knife again,

concentrating on smoothly slicing the thin tomato skins, and slipping their contents into the food processor. "Jenny is almost four. Her birthday is the next month after yours, in November. And she has a new baby brother. His name is John Benjamin but we call him J.B."

"Can I see them?"

"Of course. We've been invited to dinner with them next week."

"What are you gonna do next?" Christine was pointing to the tomatoes. She appeared to have lost interest in the family connections, for which Jillian was grateful.

"I'm going to puree them in here until there are only small chunks of tomato left. Then I'll pour them into a big pot, add the rest of the stuff to make it tasty—" She nodded to the seasonings "—and let it simmer. Do you like meatballs?"

Christine nodded.

"Good," Jillian said. "Me, too. I'm going to make some while the sauce is cooking."

"Can I help?"

Jillian looked up. The child was twirling a long strand of blond hair, studiously avoiding her eyes. How many times had this little girl's questions been ignored? She acted as if she *expected* to be refused.

"Sure," she said. "The quicker I teach you to cook, the sooner you can do it instead of me."

Christine smiled, a tentative expression that told Jillian the little girl was dying to giggle but was simply too inhibited. Wondering exactly what the child's mother had done to make her so anxious to fade into the wallpaper, Jillian made up her mind to ask Dax for details at the next opportunity.

"You never told me you could cook." The deep voice startled them both.

"You never asked." Aware of Christine's straining ears, she kept her tone light and matter-of-fact.

"Your kitchen in the condo looked like it doesn't get used much." His voice was normal enough.

She opened the refrigerator and got out a package of ground beef. "It doesn't. I eat out a lot." There, let him imagine her dining out with a different man every night. "Just because I don't cook doesn't mean I can't," she added. "I'm actually a fairly decent cook."

"I guess cooking for one isn't much fun." There was an edge in his voice.

Fine. If he wanted to throw down the verbal gauntlet, she'd be glad to pick it up.

"I wouldn't know, since I rarely cook just for myself," she said. "Most of the meals I prepare are small, intimate dinners."

"From now on, the only meals you'll be preparing are family ones."

"You must be sure of that since you seem to think it's necessary to remind me." She gave him a mocking smile. He didn't trust her anyway, so why not live up to his expectations?

"Don't push me, Jillian."

"Who's pushing? You can leave the kitchen any time you—"

"*Stop it!*" The hoarse demand came from the corner of the kitchen and they both whirled, shocked out of their animosity. Christine had pushed herself as far into the corner as she could without becoming part of the woodwork.

"Baby, it's okay. Daddy and Jillian—" But Dax never got to finish the sentence.

Launching herself out of the corner with a mighty push, the little girl raced from the kitchen. As her pounding footsteps echoed down the hall and up the stairs to the second floor, they heard the sobbing begin.

Jillian turned to Dax. "This living arrangement is going to make us all crazy." Aching to comfort the sobbing girl, she gripped the edge of the counter to keep herself from going after her. *It's not your problem,* she told herself. *She's not your kid, remember?*

Dax sat heavily on one of the tall stools at the island bar. "She's usually a little trooper. But I guess she thought we were fighting and it probably scared the hell out of her. Libby's husband shouted at her all the time in the past few years."

"At *Christine?*" She stared at him, sympathy rising. "Good Lord. You could have told me. At least I would have been a little more sensitive."

"I'm sorry. I should have warned you." His face was a study in sadness and frustration and his wide shoulders slumped wearily. "I'll go after her."

"No, I'll go talk to her. She already knows you love her. I'm the one she needs reassurance from." As Dax's head came up and he stared at her, she didn't know who was more surprised. Why in the world had she said that? She didn't want the responsibility for his child. Still, she'd said it and she'd endure torture before admitting to him that she'd made a mistake.

"Jillian?"

She had started through the swinging door but paused and looked back.

"I'm sorry." Dax's voice was subdued but sincere. "I shouldn't have picked a fight."

"I'm sorry, too," she said. "I promise you I will never raise my voice to her. And you and I are going to have to agree to keep our differences to ourselves until we have privacy to duke it out."

He smiled, as she'd intended. "I don't worry about how you treat Christine. I know you would never do anything to hurt her."

She went on up the stairs then, but inside her there was a warmth that gave spring to her steps.

That might have been the nicest compliment he'd ever given her.

The following Tuesday was the monthly meeting of Piersall's board of directors. Dax arrived early and went to his office for a final review of the materials he intended to present. He'd been in and out of the building throughout the week before, acquainting himself with Charles's staff and reviewing procedures, checking inventory and familiarizing himself again with the process of manufacturing the steel beams that the company produced.

He'd grown up here, had been groomed for a position managing the company, but his father had died when Dax was seventeen, and a hired C.E.O. had stepped in while Dax went to college. Dax had stayed in school for two additional years to complete his graduate work and had planned to come home and gradually take over the reins after that.

He'd also planned to come home and marry Jillian, but neither of those plans had materialized. When he'd been betrayed by his brother and his fiancée, he hadn't been able to get away from Butler County fast enough.

Charles, apparently, had been expected to become the company's standard-bearer, but from what he could see, Charles had been a paper figurehead, leaving most of the decisions as well as the day-to-day management in the hands of the board of directors and the employees. So far, he'd read minutes from the past three years' worth of board meetings, and it appeared Charles had missed more meetings than he'd attended.

He, Dax, had no intention of being an invisible presence.

The door of the conference room was open and he strode in. More than a half dozen men and one silver-haired

woman were seated around the table. All rose at his entrance and introductions began. Roger Wingerd was there,
neat piles of printouts stacked in front of him for distri-
bution to the board. Several of the men were longtime
stockholders he'd known before he left, and one, Gerard
Kelvey, had been a friend of his father's. Two others were
young, shrewd-eyed, ambitious-looking types. The woman
was another person he recognized. Naomi Stell's husband
had held stock, and Dax learned that since his death three
years ago, Naomi had become active on the board.

The chairman of the board banged his gavel amid the
chatter and the meeting was called to order.

And then the door opened.

Everyone turned automatically to see who else was at-
tending the meeting. No one looked away as Jillian appeared in the doorway.

She paused for a moment, and Dax unconsciously held
his breath, releasing it only when she stepped forward. She
was wearing a stylish navy suit with bold brass buttons that
fit her perfectly—too perfectly—managing to look risqué
without revealing a single hint of cleavage. The skirt of the
suit was shorter than he thought was appropriate for a business meeting, but he doubted a man there would object.
Her navy pumps made her legs look even longer, her ankles
even trimmer, and when she walked in the high heels, the
muscles in her calves and along her shins slipped rhyth-
mically beneath her silky skin. Her blond hair was tousled
artfully, a current style which should have looked sloppy
and disheveled, but on Jillian managed to give the impression of being natural and sexy as hell.

Her eyes sparkled as she looked around the room and
her reddened lips parted in a smile that displayed her perfect white teeth. As one, every man in the room rose, himself included.

Dax was the first to recover. He stepped forward and

pulled back the empty chair next to his. His brain was starting to function again, and he realized that her presence here probably meant trouble for him. If so, he wanted her where he could manage her if he needed to.

"Miss Kerr! An unexpected pleasure!" The chairman of the board beamed at her as she took the seat without glancing at Dax, and everyone else resumed their seats as well. Then, as if he remembered where he was, the man said, "It's always good to see you, of course. How may we help you today?"

Jillian waved a hand languidly in the air. "You all just go on and ignore me. I'm just here to watch and learn." Obviously, she had expected the lack of comprehension evident on everyone's face, because she added, "Charles left his stock to me, so I'll be joining you on a regular basis now."

There was a sudden, electric stillness in the room. The chairman cleared his throat. He glanced at Roger Wingerd, who spread his hands helplessly. "We, ah, were given to understand that the majority share of stock was staying in the Piersall family," the chairman said.

"And it is." Dax spoke, trying not to grit his teeth. Damn her! He should have known she'd do something to undermine his position if she could. "Jillian is *Mrs. Piersall* now. We were married last week."

"But, of course, Dax knew I would want to be an active part of any company decision-making policy." Jillian laid a graceful hand on his and turned her high-voltage smile his way. And if it held a suspicious hint of amusement, he doubted anyone else noticed.

He resisted the urge to clasp her fingers and squeeze until she begged for mercy but before he could think of a suitable comment, the surprise rippling around the room quieted as the chairman stood.

"On behalf of us all, allow me to offer congratulations

and the very best to you both,'' he said formally. As Jillian inclined her head graciously, the man tilted his reading glasses higher on his nose and directed his attention back to the agenda.

Dax was on tenterhooks throughout the whole damned meeting, wondering what she was up to. Several times she asked questions, intelligent, thoughtful questions, nodding at the answers, and he could see her filing the information away in her brain.

When the new business opened, he took the floor. He had requested this opportunity to speak, and he made the most of it, sharing his concerns about the company's shaky financial footing and outlining the proposals he favored for regaining a more solid financial picture. He fielded questions from the other board members, ignoring Roger, who was looking distinctly green around the gills as he realized his job might be in jeopardy.

''But we can't just start firing people,'' objected Naomi.

''I have no intention of just firing people,'' Dax told her. ''But there may be some layoffs necessary in the business office. Structurally, we are simply too top-heavy right now. I would like the board to vote to allow me to step into a leadership role, into the position of President held first by my grandfather and father and most recently by my brother Charles.'' As far as Dax was concerned, it was a mere formality, since he—or at least, he and Jillian—held more than fifty percent of the stock.

Then a horrible suspicion presented itself. He glanced at Jillian, listening attentively at his side. She'd told the board Charles had left his shares to her. *Did she think she was going to vote them?*

As the rest of the board began to buzz with comments among themselves, he moved his foot to one side and kicked Jillian beneath the table.

She turned and regarded him with a patient smile, a smile that confirmed his worst fears.

"I assumed I'd vote for our whole family," he murmured to her.

She hesitated as if she had never considered that. "Oh, I don't know," she said. "Charles placed his faith in me when he trusted me with his business. I feel obligated to keep an active hand in any decisions the board makes."

"Damn it, Jillian!" He wanted to pound the table in frustration. "If I don't straighten things out soon, it's going to be too late to save this company. You have to vote with me."

"Dax." She patted his hand. "I don't *have* to do anything." She paused, and he seethed at the smug look on her face. She had him over a barrel and she knew it! Then she spoke again. "But if it sets your mind at ease, I think I agree with you. Piersall needs strong, assertive leadership, and—" she smiled in wry understatement, "You have those qualities."

He turned his palm up, capturing her hand in his and squeezing gently as the tension eased out of him. "Thank you."

When the time came for the vote to be taken on his proposal, Dax was gratified to see that more than eighty percent of the stockholders backed him. Naomi Stell voted against, and to his surprise, so did Gerard Kelvey.

But as the board adjourned and he escorted Jillian out of the conference room, he couldn't prevent the small flare of pleasure deep inside. She had backed him! She trusted his judgment and she had reinforced his position with the rest of the board.

The glow faded as he recalled her claim that he had never accorded her the same trust.

Six

September wore on, and Dax was relieved to see Christine losing some of her moodiness. She liked school—thank God—and had made some friends. It seemed every time he turned around someone was dropping off or picking up a little girl who'd come to play.

Jillian, too, seemed to have settled in since her arrival two weeks ago. She spent most of her time in the evenings with Christine. In the mornings, she was out the door as soon as she'd woken the child and fixed her hair, leaving him to make breakfast and get Christine to school.

It was an arrangement that seemed to work well. The hair thing had been driving him crazy. Christine had been so reluctant to get it cut that he hadn't been able to force himself to make her, but he was totally incapable of creating ponytails and braids. Until Jillian came, it had been a long, loose mop. She took the time every morning to fix it in some pretty style with ribbons that matched the outfit they'd chosen the night before.

But she hadn't spoken to him, alone, in more than a week. He suspected she was avoiding him on purpose.

Three mornings a week she left the house at seven-thirty to go to the gym, and from there she went straight to work. Three other mornings, she refused breakfast, snatched a piece of toast and ate it as she climbed into her red Porsche and zipped away, leaving him with an impression of flying legs that went clear up to her waist, and a stirring arousal that he fully intended to do something about. Soon.

The only thing that pleased him about the situation was that she seemed to be forging a tentative friendship with Christine. A few nights ago, he had followed the sounds of giggling to the open door of Jillian's room, where he'd caught Jillian lying across the bed while his daughter tried on various items of clothing and shoes.

And so, on Saturday, he was waiting for Jillian on the landing in the morning. "I want to talk to you," he said as she quietly shut the door of her room behind her.

She jumped a full foot in the air, and came down scowling. "That'll give me gray hair."

The image brought a smile to tug at the corners of his mouth. "You? Never. You'll die a blonde, even if it comes from a bottle."

She glared at him for a moment, then relaxed enough to smile back. "You're probably right." Then she glanced at her watch. "I have to get going. What did you want?"

You. But he only said, "A couple of things. I want to host a dinner party for eight next Saturday night. Will that suit?"

She assessed him. "You've already invited them, haven't you? So why does it matter if it suits me?"

He put his hands in the air in a gesture of surrender. "Guilty. I already invited them. If you're tied up, I'll take them to the club."

She waved a hand. "Forget it. Isn't that what I was hired

for? I'll take care of it. Just find out if anyone is allergic to shellfish, and make sure I know their names before they arrive.''

"Thank you." He regarded her for a minute, irritated but not quite knowing the reason why. She'd said she'd help, hadn't she? "Christine's birthday is on the thirteenth."

"The thirteenth of October? Two weeks from now?"

"Yes. I was wondering if you could help me arrange the kind of day she might enjoy, think about what gifts I ought to get, that sort of thing."

She hesitated, then appeared to come to some decision. "Sure. I'd be glad to help you. We can talk about it tonight. After Chrissy goes to bed we can make some plans."

"Thank you. I really appreciate it."

There was an awkward silence. She was wearing a leotard with a pair of baggy sweats, and the exercise bra beneath pressed firmly against her breasts, creating cleavage that he couldn't keep his gaze away from. She shifted position, shrugging her bag higher over her shoulder, and the flesh shifted—

Then she raised her eyebrows. "What else?"

What else? He felt warmth creeping up his neck. Right. He was supposed to be talking. "Uh, I about the company—I've got some strange things going on in the books I've been looking over. If I bring them home tonight, would you look over them and tell me what you think?"

"I guess so. How about if I hold dinner for you and we can all eat together?"

"I'd like that. Our first meal as a family." He had to clear his throat, hoping she didn't see the rush of emotion in his eyes. Was it unmanly to admit that the thought of coming home to a wife and child and warm meal was powerfully appealing? He didn't think he cared.

She glanced at her watch. "I have to get going. See you tonight."

As she bounded down the steps, a door opened behind him. "Daddy? What's wrong?" Christine opened her door and looked out, shielding her eyes against the bright light in the hallway.

He turned and walked to her.

"Nothing," he said, smiling at her tousled hair and the too-big T-shirt that read, *You have to kiss a lot of frogs before you find your prince.* On the front was a big bullfrog puckered up for a kiss. "Nice shirt."

She glanced down at herself. "It's Jillian's."

"Why are you wearing it?"

"I told her I liked it and she gave it to me." Christine yawned. "It's too early. I'm going back to bed."

"Want a lift?" He held out his arms.

"Yeah!" As she reached for him, Dax bent and lifted her into his arms. She twined her arms and legs around him and laid her head on his shoulder, and he kissed her hair as he carried her back into her bedroom.

"I love you, baby."

"I love you too, Daddy."

He paused. "Did I hear Jillian call you 'Chrissy?'"

"Um-hmm. Like Mommy did when I was little. I told her she could if she wanted to." And his daughter snuggled down beneath the bedspread he pulled over her and closed her eyes. As he left the room, he rubbed a hand over his heart, trying to soothe the ache that had appeared. Christine clearly hungered for the love of a mother. If Jillian left as she insisted she would, Christine was going to be shattered.

She wouldn't be the only one.

The little girl had been invited to go to a local amusement park with a friend's family later in the morning. After he dropped her off, he went in to work for a while. Saving Piersall was proving to be a full-time job, and he was relying more and more on his manager in Atlanta to make the day-to-day decisions for Travers. *For the right offer,*

I'd sell the damn coffin company and quit making myself crazy, he thought as he pulled into the garage at seven-thirty that evening.

Then he realized what he'd just been thinking. Was he really considering selling the business in Atlanta? And coming...home, to live? Permanently? He wondered when he'd begun to think of Butler County as home again.

True to her word, Jillian had waited with the evening meal. To his delight, it went pretty smoothly. Not a prickle or a smart comment to be heard. If he hadn't been fighting his body's reaction to his wife all evening, it even would have been relaxing. As it was...one particular part of his body had no intention of calming down.

Jillian had changed from her work clothing into a T-shirt and denim shorts. The T-shirt was oversized and should have looked like a sack. On any other woman, it would have.

On Jillian...man, oh man. The fabric was faded and worn from a million washings, and it skimmed down over her breasts, catching on the tips and outlining the gentle mounds every time she made a move. The shorts were just that—short. They barely peeked out beneath the long hem of the shirt, exposing her shapely legs and giving the impression that she wore nothing beneath the shirt.

She might be an untrustworthy witch and he was probably crazy for getting involved with her again, but he sure was glad she was living in his house right now. He could barely keep his mind on Mrs. Bowley's tasty baked chicken.

Jillian talked a little about some funny things that happened at the toy store, and he forced himself to pay attention. She also drew out Christine, who chattered nonstop about her day at the park, her school and her friends once she got started. Jillian responded to her with such complete attention that he realized how little he really listened to his daughter. Guilt rose. He should have been doing this with his child on a daily basis, but it had taken a third person to make him see it.

Well, guilt could run the rest of his life if he let it. *Forget it,* he told himself. *You can't go back, but you can go forward on the right foot this time.*

They finished the meal and everyone helped clear the dishes. As Jillian loaded the dishwasher, he gave his daughter's shoulders a gentle squeeze. "I enjoyed this. I'll have to try harder to get home to have dinner with my girls."

Chris turned a shining face up to him. "That would be really nice, Daddy," she said. A beeping noise made them both glance down at a small oval disk hanging from her belt. As she squealed and detached it, he asked, "What's that?"

Christine was busy punching buttons on the face of the thing, and Jillian glanced up. She was bending over the dishwasher and he didn't know whether to be relieved or disappointed that her bottom was turned away from him. "It's a virtual pet."

"A *what?*"

"A virtual pet. They were all the rage in Japan a couple of years ago. It's a sort of game that lasts a month or more."

"You're kidding." A game that lasted a month or more?

"Nope." Jillian pointed at the little gadget. "Show him, Chrissy."

For the next ten minutes, he learned more than he ever wanted to know about the rigors of taking care of the little computerized critter. Christine's was a kitty, she explained. It needed to be fed and played with, disciplined, bathed and changed regularly. It required medicine when it got sick and the lights had to be turned out when it took naps and at bedtime.

He couldn't believe it. "This is like having a baby. You're on call all the time."

Christine nodded. "Mine sleeps all night, but it gets awake at seven in the morning, and it's hungry and sad. I have to feed it and play with it first thing."

He shook his head, bemused. "This is the craziest thing I ever heard of. We never had anything like that when I was a kid."

"Hot Wheels cars and Spiderman were the 'in-thing' back then," Jillian reminded him.

"And you played with those dumb trolls until their hair fell out."

"They were not dumb!" She flicked a dishtowel at him. "And having a troll's hair fall out was a very traumatic experience. It marked me for life."

"Right. You were *much* more careful with Barbie and Ken. They're the ones you operated on. I'll never forget your face when your mom explained that Barbie's leg wouldn't heal again after you cut it off."

"You know an awful lot about each other," Christine observed.

Silence, awkward silence, fell.

Finally, Jillian said, "I guess we do, don't we?"

Christine appeared oblivious to the sudden tension in the atmosphere. "I have to go finish my math. I *hate* homework!" She started out of the kitchen.

Jillian glanced at her watch. "And after that, you need to hit the hay. You've had a big day."

A groan was the only answer, but they could hear her footsteps as she skipped up the stairs.

The room grew quiet again.

"Well." Jillian hung up the dishtowel and looked around. "I guess this is clean enough that Mrs. Bowley won't fuss me on Monday. I'd better go check on Christine, see if she needs help with—"

"Honey-bunch."

The old endearment fell between them, and Jillian's gaze flew to his. Then she looked down at the floor, rubbing a sneakered toe around the pattern of the rug beneath the sink. "What?"

"You know what I've just realized I missed while I was away?"

She glanced up sharply. "What?"

"Roots. Memories, and people to share them with."

Her eyes were wide and blue as a summer sky, luminous as she nodded.

"No one in Atlanta *knew* me. Does that make any sense?"

Her eyes darkened. "Yes," she said simply, looking away. "It makes a lot of sense to me."

There was an odd tone in her voice, almost a plaintive note, and he remembered her sister's accident and subsequent memory loss. "You feel alone, too."

She nodded. "I do feel alone," she repeated.

"Jillian—"

She turned back to the sink, gripping the edge with both hands. "Let's just forget it, Dax."

"I don't want to forget anything," he said, and he meant it. There'd been a lot of good times that he'd buried beneath his bitterness. He stepped closer, standing directly behind her without touching her. "I've discovered that I like remembering."

"I don't." There was such sadness in her voice that he raised his hands to her shoulders and turned her around to face him. "It's better just to forget some things."

Slowly, he drew her to him. She didn't resist, though she didn't return the embrace, either. And while the feeling of her long, lithe body against him stirred prurient interest, he knew sex wasn't what she needed right now.

Gently, he pressed her head against his shoulder, knowing an overwhelming sense of satisfaction when the rigidity left her limbs and she relaxed against him. Her arms came around his waist as he put his lips against her hair, and for long heartbeats, he simply stood in the middle of the kitchen with her in his arms.

And for the first time since he'd set foot in Butler County again, he felt as if he had truly come home.

Finally, the silence was interrupted by the squawk of the intercom. "Jillian? Could you come up here? I don't get this subtracting stuff."

They drew apart slowly, and he took her hands as their bodies reluctantly parted. "I'll go. I need to spend more time with her."

His wife nodded. "She would like that."

He wanted to say more, to talk about the feelings bouncing around inside him, but he seemed to have a talent for saying the wrong thing to her. So he dropped her hands and turned toward the door.

"By the way." Her voice made him pause and look back. "Marina extended an invitation for steak on the grill next Friday night. Christine is coming along with me." Again she looked at the pattern on the rug rather than at him. "You're invited, too, if you want to come."

His initial impulse was to refuse as he remembered the scowling features of Jillian's brother-in-law. The evening would be uncomfortable, at best. But if he wanted to spend time with Jillian.... "Thank you. I'd like that."

He came back downstairs when the math was finished and Christine was tucked into bed. Jillian passed him on the stairs, on her way up to say good night, and he said, "I'll meet you in the study."

A few minutes later, she came through the door. "She's almost asleep already."

"Big day for a little kid." He smiled fondly, then indicated the table at one side of the room. "Over here are the spreadsheets for the past year's accounts. Have a look."

She did. When she finally raised her head, her eyes were dark and concerned. "It almost looks as if prices on these products were kept low on purpose. I don't believe in gouging customers but I can't see how Piersall could make much profit with margins as slim as these."

He moved closer to her and pointed to a spot on one of the charts. As he did so, his chest pressed against her arm. She glanced up—

And didn't look away.

His breath came faster. He slipped his arms around her and pulled her to face him fully, and the erotic slide of her soft curves over his hard male flesh made him close his eyes in what was very nearly a painful rush of lust. She was his wife. Why shouldn't they share the pleasures of the marriage bed? "Honey-bunch," he murmured. "I want you."

She swallowed. "I know."

"Come upstairs with me."

She gazed up at him. Slowly, he ran his hands up her back and brought every inch of her against every aching inch of him. She licked her lips and his gaze fell to her mouth. As he lowered his head, he kept looking at that lush, pink—

"Stop." Jillian put her hand over his mouth. "This isn't what I want, Dax."

"You're a liar." He punctuated the words with kisses pressed into the palm that covered his lips. "You want me as badly as I want you."

"Maybe I do," she conceded as she backed out of his embrace. "But I don't do casual sex." Her voice was soft and filled with pain, but irritation was rising inside him and he ignored it.

"We've never had casual sex in our lives," he said. "Don't you remember—"

"I remember everything." She whirled away from him and he could see her shoulders hunch as she hugged her arms around herself.

It was such a vulnerable pose that he felt the irritation subside. "I can wait a little longer, honey-bunch. But don't keep me waiting too long. You're my wife now, and I want you in my bed."

She turned then, and the sadness in her eyes hit him like a physical slap across the face. "I'm not a possession," she said. "I'm a person. And I have feelings, too, Dax." Then she slipped out of the room.

He stood there for a moment, his body begging him to go after her while his mind puzzled over her words. What could she possibly have to feel sad about? She'd been the one to cheat on him. She'd brought all their troubles on herself. But as he turned and began to gather the account information together with self-righteous annoyance, an insistent whisper from his conscience accused, *She didn't run right out and have somebody else's baby. She never married another man.*

Was it possible she still had feelings for him? He'd thought she loved his brother. But could she still love him as well?

The following Wednesday, the bell over Frannie's shop door jingled when Jillian walked in. She used the front door when the shop was closed, but today, Frannie had yet to flip over the sign to let customers know she wasn't in, so Jillian took the opportunity to wander through the shop.

Wedding accoutrements were everywhere. Frannie's little bridal shop did a booming business, largely because of its owner's skill at designing dream dresses for a girl's big day. But she also had expanded the theme to offer everything a bride could need. And there were quite a few things a bride didn't need, but surely would enjoy, scattered around the shop as well.

One new addition caught her eye and she detoured to the glass case on the way to the work room. Frannie had displayed several dolls wearing custom-made dresses and tuxes. A small brochure beside them advertised the beauty of having a replica of your own dress to remind you always of your special day.

She'd bet a nickel that had been Deirdre's idea, and she approved. What bride would be able to resist?

Her own wedding dress was still specially preserved and packed away somewhere in the recesses of the Piersall home. *Her* home. She hadn't wanted to see the gown again, after things fell apart. It had been being altered when Dax left. When the process was complete, the shop called her to pick it up and she'd told them to throw it away.

But Dax's mother, her almost mother-in-law, dear old softy, had rushed downtown and picked up the dress, putting it on the attic of Charles's and her home when Jillian had refused to take it. "Life takes a lot of strange turns," she'd said. "You might wish you'd kept this twenty years from now."

And Jillian's thoughts had flown immediately to Dax, wondering, as always, why he had never come home.

She snorted inelegantly, pushing away the dull pain that squeezed her heart. She knew the answer to that one now.

"Something funny?"

She turned, pinning a brilliant smile into place as she embraced Frannie. "Hello, darling. How's the bridal business?"

"Hello, yourself, newlywed." Frannie's eyebrows rose as she realized Jillian hadn't answered her question, but she let it pass. "The bridal business is fine. The household, however, is a different story. Have you had chicken pox?"

"When I was five. Marina brought them home from school." She gave Frannie's shoulders a sympathetic squeeze as they turned to go through the shop into Frannie's kitchen. "But I thought kids got shots to prevent them now."

"They do," said Frannie, looking totally disgusted. "But they aren't a hundred percent effective. The doctor warned me they could still get them. They just won't be very severe. And as luck would have it, Alexa was exposed at preschool. She broke out yesterday. Of course, Ian's been exposed now, and so has the baby."

Frannie led the way into the kitchen. "I'm so glad you came, Jill. My sister-in-law came down to give me some breathing room from the kids—she's upstairs now sponging down Alexa. Ian and Brittany, bless her hyperactive little heart, both are napping."

"You know I hate to miss our Wednesday lunches." Jillian sank into a chair at the table where Frannie's assistant had a pretty fruit salad and some cucumber sandwiches waiting. "I finally hired some help to replace Marina, but I'm still working like a horse. This is my treat to myself."

"What does Dax think of you working so much?"

The question caught her off guard, and she hesitated for a moment. "I don't really know," she admitted. "We haven't discussed it. He's pretty busy, too. He barely has time for Christine, much less a wife."

"Christine seemed like a nice child." Frannie had met Chrissy the previous weekend when she'd come by to drop off a couple of chairs she'd borrowed for one of her shows at the shop.

"Oh, she is." Good, a safe topic. "I've tried to be as low-key as possible. So far, we're getting along pretty well."

"Her mother and Dax, uh, are divorced?"

"Yes. But her mother remarried and the new hubby apparently doesn't want Chrissy around."

Frannie's eyes swirled with sympathy. "Does Christine know that?"

"Oh, yes. The mother didn't bother to hide it. According to Dax, she couldn't wait to get rid of the child." Jillian speared a hand through her blond mane, shoving it back from her face.

"Jill..." Frannie, usually so forthright, seemed oddly ill at ease. "The day we helped you move, you said you were only staying for six months. Was it true?"

This *really* wasn't something she wanted to explain to her friend, but since they'd all helped her move her things, she supposed she owed her some explanation. "It's true," she said softly. "Dax has some business concerns in Butler County. I'm...working with him when he needs me and helping out with Christine."

"You're telling me this really is just a business arrangement?"

Jillian nodded. "That's about it."

"But..." Frannie was floundering. "The way he watches you... I thought for sure there were some feelings there. And if you'll forgive me for sticking my nose in where it doesn't belong, I've never seen another man who makes you light up like Dax does."

"Light up?" If it didn't hurt so much, the image would be funny. "If I light up around him, it's only because he's made me so mad I'm throwing off sparks."

"See? That's just what I mean." Frannie's eyes were a piercing green, intense and direct. "No one else ever provokes strong emotions from you unless you think someone you care about is being hurt. You have a string of suitors a mile long, but they come and go and you never blink." Her voice softened, and she added, "If Dax went, I think you'd do more than blink."

"He already left me seven years ago, a month before our wedding." The bald words tumbled out before she could leash her tongue. From a reservoir that had been leaking over its walls for weeks, treacherous tears sprang to her eyes and she caught back a drop that tried to escape.

There was an instant of shocked silence.

Then Frannie left her chair and came around the table. Without hesitation, she put her arms around Jillian where she sat, pressing Jillian's head against her stomach. "Oh, baby, go ahead and cry," she invited, rubbing her palms up and down Jillian's back.

Jillian shook her head, mortified. "I don't cry," she said into the fabric of Frannie's blouse, using it to blot the tear or two that called her a liar.

The body beneath her cheek moved and she heard a low chuckle above her head. "No, you don't, do you?" Frannie leaned back slightly, assessing her with a far too astute eye and Jillian looked away. Frannie had a habit of looking into her as if she could read exactly what was roiling around inside her head, and she didn't want anyone reading her mind right now. "Tell me what happened."

Jillian sighed. "God, you're persistent. Jack isn't kidding when he says you're worse than water dripping on stone."

Frannie smiled as she gave her friend's shoulders a final squeeze and returned to her seat, but her eyes never wavered. "Why did he leave you?"

Trust Frannie to reserve judgment until the facts were on the table. She, on the other hand, would have rushed in swinging her sword and asked questions later. "It was a stupid misunderstanding," she said, sighing. "He thought he caught Charles and me in a compromising position. He didn't, of course, but he didn't wait around to find out."

"He just *left?*" Frannie's voice showed the first hint of a strident tone. "How long ago?"

"Seven years."

"And he never came back until *now?*"

Jillian swallowed the lump that rose with the memory. "He wouldn't have come back now if Charles hadn't died." She shrugged, striving for flippancy. "It was probably for the best. If he didn't trust me any more than that, our marriage never would have lasted, anyway."

"But—but—Christine—she's got to be close to seven." Now there was the beginning of incredulous anger in her friend's tone.

"A memento of the lengths he went in trying to forget me."

Frannie was shaking her head, and Jillian could see tears forming in her eyes. Before Frannie could speak, she said, "Stop that. I've made a career out of suppressing tears, and if you start, you're liable to make me ruin my dry streak."

"If you hadn't told me this, I'd have harbored hope that there might be a reconciliation in the works," her friend confessed. "You two might strike sparks, but you also seem to be…connected."

"We've known each other most of our lives. Familiarity now, not fondness."

But as she turned the conversation firmly in another direction, she knew what Frannie meant. They did share a connection, she and Dax. Reconciliation was a strong word for the fragile tendrils that had begun to stretch between them again, but beneath all the hurt, the anger and the sorrow, there was a little corner where hope was beginning to stir.

And the gentle embrace they'd shared the night before had pushed a stick into its slumbering embers until hope lay exposed, waiting for tinder to help it grow strong and vital once more.

They went to Marina's the next Friday evening. The Bradford home was a pretty brick rancher on a large lot in an older neighborhood. Summer's last flowers still edged the walk and an oak tree shaded one side, making it look calm and serene—much like Marina, Dax thought.

Then they walked through the front door and the resemblance ended.

Pandemonium reigned. Or at least it seemed like it. They were greeted by a pre-school-aged Mexican jumping bean that Ben identified as Jenny. A big brown-muzzled dog and a little white floor mop that vaguely resembled a dog danced around and through everyone's legs. Christine, unused to animals, shrank back when the bigger dog made a beeline for her, and Jillian grabbed his collar and hauled him back.

"Major, you big fool! Give her a chance to get used to you. Marina! Come call your dogs."

Marina appeared in the doorway, blue eyes sparkling as she laughed. She carried a tiny infant in one arm and the baby was screaming with every breath in its little lungs. Handing the baby to Ben, Marina gave them a hasty welcome and disappeared with the dogs.

Christine's dark eyes were huge. "Wow!" she said. "A *real* family."

Jillian said, "Amen," in a wry tone and Dax glanced at her—and stopped for a long survey.

Jenny danced along in front of her, chattering a mile a minute as Jillian moved toward the family room Ben was indicating. She had taken the baby from Ben and was soothing it with a gentle hand rubbing the small back while she listened attentively to Jenny, and to Dax's amazement, the baby was quieting. When she finally sat down on the couch, she snuggled the child against her cheek and closed her eyes for a long moment, and he got the impression she was savoring the moment.

She obviously loved children, he thought, watching as she introduced Jenny to Christine and the older girl let the smaller one drag her off to the playroom. As he had the night he'd seen the photo of her with an infant, he wondered why she had never married, never had children of her own. She couldn't have lacked opportunity.

The mere thought of her in some other man's arms made him clench his teeth until he felt a muscle ticking along his jaw and forced himself to relax.

The evening was surprisingly pleasant. He'd expected it to be awkward, since he'd hardly bothered to make a good impression at their first meeting but Marina went to great pains to make both Christine and Dax feel comfortable. Even Ben, who clearly saw himself as Jillian's protective big brother, relaxed enough to offer him a beer and talk baseball and the Orioles' chances of winning the pennant in the play-offs.

After dinner, which was an informal affair during which Jillian took turns with Ben and Marina walking the fussy baby, the little girls went outside. Jenny assured Christine that the dogs were friendly, and Dax was surprised to see how easily his daughter had accepted these strangers. When Jillian's sister encouraged Christine to call her, "Aunt Marina," it gave him quite a jolt.

"So," said Ben as he poured coffee for all the adults, "Jillian tells us you came home to some trouble with your family's business."

Dax nodded. "That's a mild way to put it."

"What exactly does Piersall do?"

"We manufacture steel. When my grandfather started the company, its largest clients were the Baltimore shipyards. But as the years passed, the shipyards were building less and less, and when my father took over, he made a conscious effort to diversify."

"How?" Ben appeared genuinely interested as he took his seat.

"By getting into construction steel. We have several

large distributors up and down the East Coast now as well as keeping our hand in what's left of the shipyard market.'' He sighed. ''The market's strong. The company should be doing well.''

''Should be but isn't.'' Jillian handed the baby who was sleeping at last to Marina and sank into a chair opposite his. ''We've both looked over the financial records. Nothing is obviously out of place but there's been a steady drop-off in profit over the past five years.''

''As a result, stock shares go down in value.'' He hesitated, then decided he might as well voice the concern that had been niggling at the back of his mind for the past few days. ''I'm starting to wonder if there's a single person or corporation buying all the stock.''

''For what purpose?'' Ben's brow furrowed.

''It wouldn't do anyone any good,'' Jillian pointed out. ''Together, we control more than fifty percent of the voting stock.''

''I know.'' Dax spread his hands on the table and regarded his knuckles absently. ''That's what bothers me. It makes no sense.''

There was a short silence around the table. The baby, John Benjamin, smacked his lips in innocent slumber and as one, they laughed.

Then Jillian rose. ''Thanks for the meal. We'll return the invitation one of these days. Right now, we'd better get Christine out of here so you can get Jenny to bed.''

When they went to get the little girls, it was clear that Christine was in her element. He had never thought about how lonely her young life might be, but as he watched her mothering the smaller child, he realized that his daughter was having a ball. She'd be great with younger brothers or sisters.

Younger brothers or sisters. He realized what he was thinking. He'd gotten all too used to having Jillian in the house and in his life again. Now he was starting to think of long-range things—like babies.

What had happened to him since he came back?

He was all too afraid he knew exactly what, and her name was Jillian Elizabeth Kerr. *Piersall.* Jillian Piersall. He would never trust her again, and he sure as hell would never let himself love her the way he'd loved her once, but as long as he didn't let her lead him around like she did every other man who came near her, he'd have the upper hand.

He could manage her.

Seven

Dax's business dinner was scheduled for the following weekend. Jillian and Mrs. Bowley had spent every spare minute during the week cleaning every square inch of the house. Or at least, the main floor, which was a challenge in itself.

Jillian checked the liquor stock and bought a few more bottles, polished crystal and silver, and spot-cleaned the rug in the foyer where Christine had tracked in mud. She called the caterer, planned a menu and hired the bartender. She folded napkins into an attractive flower that could be set in the middle of each plate, and she ordered a box of delectable petit-fours from the bakery near Kids' Place. She had her nails done and her highlights touched up.

And on Saturday morning, she went shopping.

"Are you planning to eat with us this evening?" she asked Christine at breakfast.

The girl hesitated. "Is that okay with you and Daddy?"

"Of course it is. In fact, it would be good for you to see how these things work in case you ever have to host one someday." Christine was a little young to be worrying about hosting dinner parties but the child clearly wanted to be there, though she was too unsure of herself to say so.

"Okay," Christine said. "If you think I should, I guess I'll eat with you."

"Great. I'm going shopping for something to wear. Want to come along?"

Christine's eyes grew wide. "You don't have anything to wear?"

Jillian knew she was envisioning the walk-in closet upstairs stuffed with a far-too-extensive wardrobe. She laughed. "Yes, I have things I could wear, but it's a great excuse to get a new dress. You probably ought to get one, too."

To her dismay, Christine's eyes filled with tears. "My mother used to make my dresses before she sent me away. I still have some but they're all too small."

"Oh, honey." The child's grief touched her own sore heart and she got up from her chair and went around the table, taking Christine onto her lap and hugging her. Dax's daughter grabbed her around the neck in a stranglehold as her thin frame shook and Jillian rocked her, patting her back, reminded of the way Frannie had comforted her a few days ago.

Finally, Christine's sobs began to abate.

"I'd make you a dress," Jillian said, trying to lighten the moment, "But I can't sew worth beans. You'd look like a reject from a rummage sale."

Christine gave a hiccuping giggle. "A bag lady."

"Raggedy Ann."

Christine giggled again. She loosened her arms and lifted her head from Jillian's shoulder, slipping off her lap self-consciously. "Sorry I soaked your shirt."

"It's okay. Everybody needs a good cry now and then." Amen to that, she thought silently. She'd suppressed so many tears in recent weeks that her chest muscles felt permanently strained. She got up and went around the table, picking up her dishes.

"Tell you what," she said to the girl. "I can help you pack your dresses away in special wrapping so they'll be preserved for your own little girl to wear someday."

Christine's whole face lit up. "You can?"

"That way, you'll have some wonderful memories of your mother to share with your children."

Christine giggled, distracted from her moment of sadness. "Talking about my children sounds really weird."

Jillian shrugged. "That's me. Old Weird Jillian."

The child giggled again. Then there was a pause.

"Jill?" Christine had heard Marina call her that and had begun to use the short form of her name as well.

She turned and looked back across the table at the girl. "What?"

"I thought I was going to hate having a stepmother. But I don't."

"Good." She had to swallow the lump in her throat. "I thought I was going to hate *being* a stepmother. But it's been pretty awesome so far."

She turned around again and backed through the swinging door into the kitchen—and saw Dax standing just on the other side of the doorway. He had a smug look on his face and she could almost see him telling himself how well this arrangement was working out, what a great decision it had been to force her into this marriage.

Smacking his face was an almost irresistible impulse, but somehow she managed to brush by him. Still, she had to puncture that airbag of satisfaction somehow. "We're going shopping this morning," she said, setting her dishes in the sink. "Can we pick up anything for you? I noticed your belts and pants seemed to be getting a bit tight around the waist.''

He chuckled, and then he was behind her so fast she never saw him move. His hands settled at her waist and he dragged her back against him, nuzzling his face into her neck and biting gently. "There's not a thing wrong with the *waist* of my pants," he said. "But you're right. They are tight." His fingers splayed across her abdomen as she felt the burgeoning erection he wasn't bothering to hide pushing at her from behind. Electric currents of arousal streaked from her neck to the hidden junction between her legs; her breasts tightened so instantly that the sensation was almost as painful as it was pleasurable.

"Dax," she hissed, putting her hands over his and pulling. Getting nowhere. "Stop it. Chrissy could come through here any time."

"So?" His teeth dragged aside the neck of her shirt and he set his lips on the tender skin exposed.

She shuddered as his mouth moved back up, seizing her earlobe and sucking, intensifying the ache in her breasts and the restless sensation that urged her to move her hips. And she realized her hands no longer were trying to push him away. Instead, they had slid back to clutch him behind the thighs and pull him even closer. Without her permission.

She wrenched herself away from him. "I am *not* your sexual toy." But it wasn't the most convincing thing she'd ever said, given the way she was panting.

He smiled at her, and leaned back against the sink, crossing his arms over his broad chest, and she couldn't ignore the shape of his aroused flesh filling the front of his jeans. "I never said you were."

"And I am *not* sleeping with you."

The smile grew wider. "Okay. No sleeping." His eyes

blazed with the black fire of desire. "We never slept much, anyway."

The images his words provoked brought exciting, enticing memories with them, bombarding her resolve. If she didn't do something drastic, she was going to wind up exactly where he wanted her, and she refused to sleep with him again, knowing what he thought of her. *Knowing what he thought of her.*

Suddenly, it was no problem at all to resist him. "You think I slept with your brother."

The words burst out like bullets, and Dax's smile shattered into a razor-sharp baring of teeth. "You told me I was wrong." His arched brows dared her to prove it.

"It doesn't matter what I told you. What matters to me is that you believed I could do something like that." She backed toward the swinging door, wary of the sudden glitter of rage that leaped from his eyes. "I'll assist you with business dealings until the day six months is up, and then I'm out of here. I can't live in the same town with you." She shook her head blindly. "I won't."

She pushed through the door and ran through the dining room. Christine looked up, startled, but she kept on going. As she sped up the stairs, she heard Chrissy's voice saying, "What did you *say* to her, Daddy?"

It took a determined effort, but she calmed herself, running cold water in her bathroom and splashing her face, then washing it and reapplying her makeup.

Twenty minutes later, she knocked on Christine's door, emotions firmly shut away, feelings numbed and dull. "The shopping train is leaving. All aboard."

Dax put on his tux before he went down to check things over one last time. He hated to admit it, but he was nervous as hell. The men who would be his guests this evening could very well mean the success or the sinking of Piersall Industries.

He'd cut every cost he could, hounded negligent clients for past-due amounts and negotiated extended repayment terms with the company's creditors. But unless he brought in this big contract and convinced these bankers to back him, it wasn't going to be enough.

Oh, he could sell his own company for a cool six million tomorrow. He knew because he'd already been making some inquiries. There was an offer on the table right now. But fixing Piersall's problems with additional cash of his own didn't sit well at all. Not because he cared about sinking money into the family industry, but because if he couldn't pull this off, he'd have failed.

Failure wasn't a word he'd often needed to contemplate. In fact, he thought sourly, his broken engagement and his subsequent marriage to the wrong woman was probably the one and only big failure in his life.

The morning's confrontation had stuck in his craw all day. How, he asked himself as he descended the stairs, could *she* be so mad at *him?* He'd been the one wronged, but somehow, she'd managed to twist everything around and make him feel like the villain. And he wasn't.

Was he?

For the first time since he was twenty-seven, a shaft of uncertainty pierced the solid block of memory he'd erected in his mind. Had he misread something on that night so long ago? It was getting harder and harder to reconcile the warm, brutally honest woman he found beneath her veneer with the woman he believed had cheated on him with his own brother.

He checked his watch. Seven-oh-one. He paced. He looked in on the hired bartender and the caterers, who had everything ready to present at a moment's notice. Thanks to Jillian.

He checked his watch again. A minute, thirty seconds had elapsed. Their guests were due any minute, damn it. Where was she? He walked to the foot of the stairs and looked up.

Nothing.

He drummed his fingers on the newel post.

And then Christine came into view. "Hi, Daddy." She was wearing a drop-waisted dress with sheer, puffy sleeves and a skirt so full it bounced when she walked. Her straight blond hair had been curled in soft ringlets and caught up in a velvet bow. She looked so...so grown up.

Surely this couldn't be his baby. Hadn't he been carrying a rosy-cheeked toddler just yesterday? Where had the chubby little legs gone? As her dark lashes swept down over her big eyes, he had a sudden flash of what his daughter was going to become in just a few short years. And it made him nervous as hell.

"Do you like my dress?" Christine pranced the stairs and pirouetted before him, and suddenly his little girl was back.

"You look beautiful, baby." he told her sincerely, kissing her brow. "Too beautiful. I can see I'm going to have to lock you in your room to keep the boys away."

"Dad-dy!" She giggled, but she was pleased. Then she turned and pointed up the stairs. "Just wait 'til you see what Jillian bought."

A flash of blue teased the corner of his vision and he lifted his head. Jillian hadn't waited to pose for him at the head of the stairs. She already was descending, looking at the steps below her rather than waiting for his reaction, her slender figure moving with sinuous grace and surety despite the mile-high sandals she wore.

His blood pressure shot up again, but this time it wasn't anxiety causing the increase in his pulse. It struck him that she knew exactly how she looked and what it was doing to him, and though his hands itched to readjust himself within his close-fitting trousers to a less restrictive position, he forced himself not to move. Hardly appropriate in front of his daughter.

Jillian's dress was a soft sapphire blue, as were her strappy little shoes. It wrapped every slender curve in a touchable, mouth-watering package. A high collar of lace surrounded her neck. The same lace formed the long, close-fitting sleeves and the bottom four inches or so of the short dress, offering tantalizing glimpses of well-toned thighs in sheer, gold-sheened hosiery. Some sheer gauzy stuff pretended a modesty that didn't exist over her upper chest, caressing the upper swells of her breasts between her collar and the main part of the dress, which looked like nothing so much as blue cling-wrap molding her from the upper curves of her breasts to mid-thigh, where the lace began. Peeping through the sheer fabric, her skin appeared to drape gracefully over her collarbones, inviting a man to run his fingers along the gentle ridges and follow the shadowed valley that disappeared between her breasts.

As she completed her glide down the stairs, he stepped forward to offer his hand. She placed hers atop his and her eyes flew to his at the contact. Slowly, he drew her fingers to his lips, holding her gaze as he pressed a lingering caress to her flesh.

"The hostess isn't supposed to outshine her guests," he murmured as he straightened. He noticed she was wearing more makeup than usual, and though he liked her normal look, whatever she'd done tonight gave her a perfect glowing finish and made her eyes even wider and her lips more pouty than ever. This close, her scent invited him to come nearer, to step in for a deeper breath.

Her darkened eyebrows rose. "Everything you requested is ready," she said coolly, and his dazed brain remembered she'd been furious with him when they parted. And why.

She started to withdraw her hand, but he held on. "I apologize for this morning," he muttered. He wasn't sure why he was the one apologizing, but it felt necessary. Christine had drifted into the living room and found the candy dish.

She gave him a long, level look. "Apology accepted. Let's forget it."

"You're big on forgetting." He kept her hand in his as the doorbell rang to announce the first of their guests.

And as she moved ahead of him to welcome the others, she shrugged those elegant shoulders. "It gets me through the day."

Lingering over coffee and Grand Marnier after the meal, he glanced down the table toward where she was seated at the far end, Christine on her right. He could admit it now—he'd been a little nervous about Jillian tonight, as well. If she'd wanted to, she could have ruined the evening and his chances at keeping Piersall going, he had no doubt. The woman had more tricks up those lacy sleeves than a roomful of magicians.

But she'd been perfect. So perfect, in fact, that his dazzled dinner companions already had agreed to a sweet deal of a loan that should give him room to breathe until Piersall was out of the woods and solvent again. She'd stroked the men's egos and listened, wide-eyed, to a dozen boring stories with all the fascination she'd have given a diamond merchant offering her a deal.

But what amazed him even more was that she'd done it without alienating their wives. She'd talked cooking, asked questions about children and grandchildren, pitched her store in a way that guaranteed a visit from every woman at the table, and listened with a straight face to a long, animated discussion about gynecologists. She'd cozied up to their men, but she'd done it in such a way that their wives hadn't felt the least bit threatened.

That was part of her charm, he decided. She vamped outrageously, then laughed at herself, and in doing so, sent the message that she wasn't to be taken seriously. She'd also played the part of the proud, doting mother to perfection. Although to be fair, he didn't think she'd had to play the role.

She genuinely liked his daughter. It showed in the way she'd helped her select a dinner dress. In the way she gently squeezed her shoulders, the way she included her in conversations, the winks and warm smiles she occasionally sent Christine's way.

He'd had more than one man compliment him on his beautiful wife and daughter and the wife of the senior lender had told him his daughter was going to be as stunning as her mother when she was grown.

An easy mistake to make, he thought. They *did* look alike.

Thinking about the reason for that dampened his good spirits. Christine *should* be Jillian's daughter. Instead, her mother had been a stand-in for Jillian during the lowest period in his life.

Tonight, he decided, was as good a night as any to get some answers about that time.

Finally! Jillian turned away as Dax closed the door on the last of their all-too-ready-to-stay-later guests. While he went to tip the bartender, she checked the kitchen to be sure the caterers had put away all the food. They would send a bill over on Monday. She had to remember to tell Dax exactly what he could and couldn't deduct as business expenses for the evening's entertainment.

Wearily, she walked toward the steps and began to climb. She couldn't wait to get out of these ridiculous shoes. Although they *had* looked fantastic with the dress. Christine had seen them and practically dragged her into the store on their way out of the mall; Jillian would have bought and worn them even if she'd hated them.

The child had gone to bed two hours ago, when Jillian had noticed her little eyes were glazed over with either exhaustion or boredom. She wished she could have done the same.

Entering her bedroom, she pried the high blue heels off one by one. Then she wriggled her way out of the dress and let it lay where it fell. Next came the hose, the panties and that incredibly uncomfortable push-up bra that did such wonders for women's cleavages.

Everything stayed right on the floor where she stepped out of it. Letting her clothing languish was satisfying. Her way of thumbing her nose at the things women did in fashion's name. Tomorrow was time enough to pick up.

Entering the big tiled bathroom, she turned on the hot water in the tub and poured in a generous dollop of bubble bath. While it filled, she brushed her teeth and took off the evening makeup she'd applied hours earlier. Ready for a wonderful, relaxing soak, she turned off the faucets and was about to step into the tub when a movement in the mirror caught her eye.

Dax stood in the partially open doorway. He had been twirling her lacy bikini panties on one finger, grinning, but the smile slowly died as their eyes met in the mirror.

She swallowed, and forced herself not to cover her exposed body like some blushing Victorian virgin.

Dax's hand closed over the scrap of material he held, until the lace disappeared beneath his fisted fingers. His gaze left hers, devouring every inch of her naked body as blotches of deep, ruddy color stained his cheekbones. His chest rose and fell visibly.

"Come here," he said, so low it was only a guttural whisper.

Come here. He was giving her the choice.

She knew what he wanted from her. There was no love for her in his heart anymore. It would be strictly a sexual thing, albeit an exclusive one legally sanctioned by their recent vows.

If she walked across the tiled floor and stepped into his arms, she would be committing herself to Dax in the most intimate way of all, knowing full well what he believed of her. And, although he would never know it, she would be unlocking her heart to him again, giving him her love even though it wouldn't be returned.

She had never stopped loving him.

Never. The admission lifted her feet, propelled her across the room step by slow step, until she was standing directly before him. Her nipples were taut with the tension she sensed in him, and there was a low throbbing between her thighs. Standing naked before him while he was fully clothed was erotic in itself, giving her a breathless vulnerability that quickened her breathing to match the air whistling in and out of his lungs.

"Jillian," he said hoarsely. "I want you."

Slowly, she raised her arms to his black-clad shoulders. "Then you can have me," she said quietly.

And that quickly, she was engulfed. His arms came around her as his mouth came down, one hand gripped the curve of her bottom, the other arm formed an inescapable bar of muscled strength beneath her back, clasping her tightly against him and bending her backward beneath his wild, demanding kiss. She speared the fingers of one hand through his hair, loving the perfect feel of his skull beneath her hand as his hot mouth ravaged hers, giving and taking in a sensual dance of passion promised.

His lips traveled down her throat, unerringly seeking her breast and she jolted and cried out when he fastened his mouth on one sensitive tip, suckling so strongly that her knees buckled, and he took the full weight of her slender body. The fierce assault sent straight shafts of desire from her nipple to her womb, so overwhelming that she whimpered into his hair. Immediately, his mouth gentled, and he murmured against her tender skin, "I don't want to hurt you."

"You're not. It's just—just…"

"I know." His voice sounded incredibly tender and tears sprang to her eyes. This was the man who'd loved her once. The man her heart remembered.

He was everywhere, suckling, licking, stroking, his hand sliding over the smooth flesh of her back and waist and hip with sweet surety. She arched under his petting, aching for more, and his hands grew even bolder, traveling unerringly down into her aching cleft of feminine need. His fingers were rough at first, abrading her most tender flesh, but soon they were bathed with the moisture that she felt flooding between her thighs.

Dax groaned as his fingers explored her and he found the slick, moist heat waiting for him. Her thighs closed instinctively over his hand and she moaned at the feel of his flesh trapped in such an intimate manner. He spun her, backing her against the vanity counter, lifting her hips until her buttocks were supported on the counter and her legs were spread wide around him. His mouth came back to hers and he slanted his lips across hers, fusing their mouths in a long, sweet kiss that spoke of more than simply the pleasures of the flesh.

Wanting, needing the ultimate intimacy they'd once shared, she slipped her hand between them and her palm stroked down over the fabric of his dress pants to cradle the long, full bulge of his arousal. He jerked, and groaned into her mouth and she pressed her palm firmly against him, moving her hand up and down over his tumescent flesh beneath the fabric.

His breathing rasped loud and fast in the silence of the

room, and she felt the sudden increase in his urgency. He held her head in one big palm, kissing her deeply and between her legs she felt his hand impatiently moving hers aside and jerking down his zipper, shoving aside rough layers of fabric that brushed her inner thighs, and suddenly, shockingly, she felt him, hot, bold and ready, pressing against her nest of dewed curls.

He drew back a fraction, finding her slick channel and moving himself into position, wrenching his mouth from hers to mutter, "I have to have you," and then he lifted her hips in his grip and plunged into her.

She was so wet and wanting that he slid into her very center with his first thrust. She screamed and bucked against him, and without giving her a second to relax or prepare, he took her on a fast, jolting journey of pleasure that tightened her body into a helpless vessel of need, arching her back as he pounded frantically against her most sensitive flesh. She cried out and he covered her mouth with his own again, drinking her cries, then leaving her mouth to throw his head back as he increased the speed of his thrusts. She pressed her mouth to his strong throat and savored the sensations bombarding her, feeling her body heating and boiling, pushing her higher and higher until the mounting coil within her sprang free and she shuddered into breathless convulsions that milked his hard flesh. He shouted then, an incoherent sound of satisfaction, and gripped her hips so that he could move even more surely within her, until his body tightened and his back arched, and with a final groan of overwhelming pleasure, he followed her into release.

He poured himself into her again and again, his bursts of power decreasing until they both were gasping like winded racehorses, her forehead propped against his chest, his chin resting on her hair. His arms were shaking and below their still-joined bodies, she could feel the long muscles in his legs quivering as well.

She started to draw back, but he pulled her closer. "Stay here." And wrapping his arms beneath her hips, he staggered with her to the pretty queen-sized bed. He pivoted so that he went down first, on his back, keeping her with him and around him.

She kissed his throat above the starched collar he'd tugged open after the guests had gone. "That was pretty smooth."

"Um-hmm." He sounded as content as a lion whose huntresses had just brought him his meal. "That's me, smooth as silk." He ran one hand from the ball of her shoulder down past the indentation of her waist and the swell of her hip. "You're pretty smooth, yourself."

Feeling her strength returning, she slowly shoved herself into a sitting position and went to work on the studs of his shirt. "This has got to go."

He raised his head far enough to look down at himself, still fully dressed with her perched on his hips, and his chest rose and fell in silent amusement. "I agree." Rolling to his side, he gently disengaged himself from her, giving a grunt of displeasure as they separated, surging to his feet in one lithe, graceful move.

Lying where he'd left her, she watched as he removed his clothing, revealing the sheets of muscle his workouts created, the strong shoulders and the cloud of black hair that thinned to a dark, silky arrow as it reached his groin, only to blossom thick and curly around the masculine flesh that still displayed the full strength of his desire.

In another minute, he reached for her, pulling back the covers and laying her on the sheet, joining her after turning out the lights. She sighed with a long-denied pleasure he echoed when their naked bodies slid against each other for the first time in seven long years, and he dragged her beneath him, pressing her knees wide and finding his niche between her thighs. "I think," he told her, "I'm going to have to scratch this seven-year-itch again."

"It feels like you're doing more than thinking about it," she said, shifting her hips against him.

She reached down between them and guided him into her, and he dropped his head and kissed her. This time, the kiss was long and sweet and slow, and she was writhing beneath him before he finished. When he raised his head, he said, "Why does it feel so right with you? You got into my head every time I did this with another woman."

She closed her eyes, turning her head aside as shafts of pain splintered and sliced her heart. She'd had two lovers, far less than the world supposed, in the years since he'd left, both utterly forgettable. So she shouldn't be so bent out of shape. But the thought of him...

He took her chin in his hand, gently stroking her cheek and turning her back to face him again. "There's never been anyone for me but you. I tried to forget you, but I always dreamed we'd be together again some day."

The words were a soothing balm, and she raised her hands to trace the strong lines of his face as he slowly began to move within her. "I know," she said simply. "It was the same for me."

She fell asleep in his arms just before dawn.

God, but she felt good in his arms. Right. She felt *right*. He was sorry he'd brought up other women. The warm satisfaction had drained from her eyes and he'd seen the hurt that was left.

He knew how that felt.

Jeez. Had he said that bit about the others to punish her? He hadn't done it consciously. But suddenly he doubted himself. He'd carried so much bitterness around for so long that maybe he couldn't judge his words or actions fairly.

Angling his head down, he pressed a kiss to the side of her cheek. The caress made her stir in his arms and he ran his palm over her back, pulling her more closely against him. She was lying against his left side, breasts pressed against him with her left leg drawn up and over his hip. He pulled her leg higher, mildly amazed at the renewed stirring in his loins as her warm flesh skimmed over him.

Men were supposed to be at their sexual peak a good decade or more younger than he was. But other women had never made him react this way. He'd forgotten just how potent her effect on him was. He'd never had such an insatiable need to sink himself into another woman, to stamp her with his brand and make her his completely. Sex without her was only sex, usually a one-time, "How-soon-can-I-politely-leave?" deal.

So what was sex with Jillian?

Chemistry, he decided. Simple chemistry. For whatever reason, she was the only woman who tripped all the right switches. Always had been, always would be.

He might as well face it, he didn't want to spend the rest of his life without her warm, soft presence in his bed every night.

No matter what she'd done.

But suddenly, the image he hated, the image that had chased him through the years and back here to his brother's funeral, came into full focus. Jillian and Charles. He couldn't help it—the mental picture that sprang onto his internal movie screen made him want to shake her awake and shout at her.

So you can piss her off and have her leave again? Not smart, Dax. If you can't have it all, at least you can have her body. Which is all you really want any more, anyway.

Wasn't it? He pushed away the memory of a tender embrace in the kitchen, an embrace that had spoken little of passion and much of other emotions.

She stretched and stirred again, shoving her tousled blond hair out of her face and lifting her head from the crook of his arm. Her blue eyes were like a sleepy cat's, blinking as if to protest being awakened from a good nap, and she raised a hand to caress his cheek. "Can't sleep?"

"Nope." He pulled her up to rest on his body and she smiled against his shoulder, automatically parting her legs for him as she felt the evidence of his body's reaction trapped between them. "I think I need something to help me nod off."

"I've never met a man who needed so much help to get to sleep." Her voice was teasing.

Oh, yeah? How about my brother? "You never did tell me why you were in bed with Charles."

The words came out of nowhere, surprising him as much as they did her. Dax made his voice as casual as possible, but it was liked he'd zapped her with a cattle prod.

Her body went rigid for an instant, and before he could catch her, Jillian slipped through his hands and practically leaped from the bed. She walked to her closet and grabbed a robe, stuffing her sleeves into the arms and tying the silk belt with a vicious tug.

He sat up, ignoring his nudity, and then got up to stand on the opposite side of the bed as she walked back, staring at him with hot, angry eyes.

"Was this supposed to soften me up so I'd confess my sins?" She jerked her head toward the bed.

He spoke slowly, trying to keep his voice from betraying any emotion. "Of course not. But I think I deserve an answer. I've always wondered why you agreed to marry me if you wanted him."

Slowly, she crossed her arms and rubbed her palms up and down her upper arms. "You've never been interested in hearing my side of the story before, Dax. Why bother after all this time?"

"You know why." He pitched his voice low and seductive.

"You mean because we just had sex?" In contrast, her tone was flat. "I'm not stupid enough to think that changes anything."

A disquieting flash of fear snagged and caught on her words. "It changes things for me," he said. He hadn't intended to open this can of worms, had planned to be content with what he had. But something within him desperately needed closure.

She raised her eyebrows, then bit her lip and looked away and he could see she was silently doubting him. Sadness flooded her eyes and he could hardly bear the pain seared into them, though her face was a smooth marble mask. "There was a time when I would have told you everything…a time when I waited and *waited* and waited for you to come home so I could tell you. But you never came, Dax."

He could see the devastation that still haunted her lurking behind her stoic facade.

"You never came."

"I couldn't." He offered the only defense he had. "I was so angry I'd have killed you and Charles both if I'd come home. It took me years to get past it. Hell, I *still* get mad."

But she was shaking her head. "That doesn't convince me. You and I both know your undying love for me washed away in the first big storm we had. You didn't trust me enough to believe in me. You didn't come home because you were too busy seducing other women and making a baby." Her voice shook and she stopped abruptly, biting her lower lip.

The truth rose like the inexorable advance of the tide, sweeping away all the excuses, all the pretenses he'd clung to all these years, and he found he couldn't let her go on thinking the worst of him.

"I stayed away," he said quietly, "Because you had torn my heart out and ripped it apart. It took me a long time to patch it back together and it hasn't worked right since." His voice was hoarse and he walked around the bed and took her hand, needing to hold it, to hold her. "We can't change the past. But we can forget it."

"We can't ignore the past, Dax. We have to face it."

"No, we don't." He drew her to him and put his index finger beneath her chin, celebrating silently when she didn't pull away. "Let's start fresh here and now. Pretend we just met."

She was silent, her eyes cast down so that he couldn't guess at her thoughts. As if she truly was shaking off the past, she gave a convulsive shiver. But then she looked up, and a teasing sparkle dropped down to mask the shadows in her eyes.

She put out her hand and wrapped small, soft fingers around his still-erect flesh, and he closed his eyes on a groan. "For two people who just met, we seem to have gotten to know each other awfully well."

Eight

The next Thursday was Christine's seventh birthday. Jillian had planned the party to take place right after school, and as she placed the cake with its frosting decorated in the figure of a popular doll on the dining room table, she glanced at her watch.

"Eek! It'll soon be three-thirty. I think we're almost ready. Run upstairs and get the gifts, will you?" She eyed Dax's efforts as he stepped down from the chair on which he'd been standing. The dining room had been transformed into a pink-and-lavender crepe-paper-and-balloons party room, and finally, she thought she was satisfied with the number of twists she'd had to give that last streamer to make it drape the right way.

As Dax left the room, she allowed herself a single wistful glance at his broad-shouldered form. She'd slept in his bed for the past five nights now, and if all she cared about was physical gratification, she'd be a deliriously happy woman.

Dax was a superb lover. He knew exactly where to touch her and when. In their years apart he'd acquired polish and control, and the result was that she was beginning to get circles under her eyes from lack of sleep. They matched the ones beneath his.

But as shattering as their sexual relationship was, there was still an ache around her heart that refused to leave.

They had talked about a million things in the past few days. He wanted her help planning a surprise trip to Disney World for Christine, he had asked her opinion on a complete renovation of the house's dated kitchen, and they'd discussed cost-saving strategies for the company. He'd even asked her to be present when he interviewed for a new office manager to replace the person who had quit when all the changes in her routine proved to be too much.

The one thing they hadn't talked about, though, was the one thing that mattered most to her. And because they hadn't, she was very careful to make no plans for a future with him. Day to day, that's all she could expect, and she wasn't going to let herself forget it.

He'd never allowed her to talk about their past, about what had really happened the night he left. And despite the tenderness and care with which he showered her, she knew they never could grow as close as she wanted, could never share a future, without exorcising that past.

He still didn't believe her. He'd told her he was willing to forget, to forgive. Her first instinct had been to kick him where it would count, her second to leave. But her love for him had held her fast.

She'd known life without him once, and she simply couldn't do it again. But this time, she promised herself, she wasn't going to expect anything. This was her choice. Even though he didn't love her, even though she knew he didn't trust her, she chose to stay. The key was expectation, she assured herself. She didn't expect him to love her. She would leave at the end of six months with memories to sustain her for the rest of her life.

She heard him coming back down the stairs and she moved to meet him, removing the top two packages from the pile he carried.

"I think you got a little carried away with the gift-buying," he said as he eyed the pile.

"You told me to go ahead and use my best judgment," she reminded him. "You should know better than to send me on a shopping spree. I take shopping as a serious mission."

He grinned, rolling his eyes as he took her hand and pulled her toward him. "Some things never change."

She allowed him to draw her against him. Her body yielded and her breath caught in her throat when he ran his hands down her back and cupped the soft globes of her bottom, pulling her up against him. It simply wasn't fair, this instant response that he, and he alone, could call from her.

The fact that she seemed to have the same effect on him was beside the point.

"Thank you for planning this," he said above her head. "I wouldn't have had a clue."

"I know," she said smugly. She kissed his jaw and ran her lips down his neck to the hollow of his throat.

He groaned. "What do you think you're doing?"

"Just playing." She smiled against his neck as she laid her head against his shoulder. Touching him whenever, however, she liked, was a pleasure she hadn't gotten used to yet.

"That's what I was afraid of," he said, chuckling ruefully.

"You started it," she reminded him. And then the doorbell rang as the first children began to arrive, and she stepped away from him, flicking her hair back and smoothing his shirt. "Are you ready to party?"

"Why do I think my idea of a party isn't quite what you have in mind this afternoon?" he asked rhetorically as he followed her through the house.

On Friday, Jillian got home from Kids' Place early. To her surprise, Dax's car already was parked in the garage, and she hurried through the back door to find him. As she walked through the kitchen, the telephone rang.

She hesitated, grimaced, and picked it up. "Hello?"

"Jillian?"

"This is she."

"Hello. It's Roger. Roger Wingerd."

"Hi, Roger." Her voice warmed. She genuinely liked Roger. He'd been a good friend to Charles and she'd dated him a few times. She'd been glad when Dax told her he hadn't felt it necessary to eliminate Roger's position.

"Um, Jillian, would you have a drink or dinner with me tomorrow?"

"Tomorrow? Tomorrow's Saturday. And Roger, now that Dax and I are married, I don't think—"

"It's business," he said. "Though I was sorry to hear you'd married him. Purely selfish," he added hastily. "Congratulations."

"Thank you." She was amused. She could only imagine what quiet, easygoing Roger thought of Dax's take-no-prisoners approach to management.

"I really do need to talk to you. As a stockholder."

"Oh. Well, I can't manage it this weekend, but Wednesday after work we probably could grab a drink. Dax has more shares than I do. Do you want him to come along?"

"No, that's all right. I'll talk to him at the office." Roger sighed dramatically. "At least give me one last shining moment with the girl of my dreams."

She laughed. "Charmer." They decided on time and location and she replaced the handset and moved on through the house to find her husband.

He was in the study, and he looked up in surprise as she paused in the door. "You must be psychic. You're just the person I want to see."

"What are you doing home?"

He waved a hand at the papers covering the top of his desk. "I brought some things home to work on. Actually, I didn't want anyone else to see what I was looking at."

She crossed the room to stand at his right side, putting an arm across his shoulders and leaning forward. "What *are* you looking at?"

"This is a list of the stock that's been bought and sold in the past few weeks. I've had a funny feeling about it, and this only adds to it." He shifted his chair to one side and pulled her into his lap, tapping the paper he pulled toward him. "I think major transactions of Piersall stock have been taking place throughout the last week couple of weeks. I hoped it was only a market fluke, a reaction to Charles's death and my appointment to the company's presidency."

She tensed at the mention of Charles, but he didn't appear to mind talking about him. Hastily, she said, "And what makes you think it's something more?"

"Here's the name of the corporation who acquired nine percent last week."

She read the small print aloud. "Shallot, Limited."

"Now look at this one." He pulled another piece of paper toward them and pointed to an underlined section. "This was from the last week in September."

"Shalott, Inc. They bought a seven percent share." She twisted to face him, bewildered. "I don't get it. Similar names?"

"I didn't get it either, until I saw this." He handed her

a third page. "This is the transaction record for this week, through lunch today."

Shalot, L.L.C. The name jumped out at her. They'd bought another five percent. "You think one corporation is behind all three of these buys?"

"It was just different enough that I overlooked it a dozen times," he said in a disgusted tone.

"So whoever this is owns twenty-one percent of the company now."

"At least," he reminded her. "We don't have any way of knowing if they hold stock in any other name as well."

She drummed her fingers on his forearm where it lay across her lap. "I still don't see what the problem is. Our family controls more than half the voting stock."

"I know." He shrugged, though she could see he was still uneasy. "But it bothers me that this is being done in such a sneaky way. Someone clearly doesn't want us— me—to see what they're up to."

"Probably because you've managed to terrify just about everyone you've met who had anything to do with managing Piersall Industries while you were gone," she said, smiling.

He snorted. "Too bad. I wouldn't have had to step in this way if it had been in a sound financial position. Speaking of sound positions..."

Startled, she glanced at him, and the look on his face telegraphed an immediate message throughout her body. Her thighs suddenly felt super-sensitive, and she was aware of the heat radiating from his flesh beneath hers.

Her body was melting. She lifted her arms and encircled his neck, bringing her breasts into contact with his chest, telling him without words that she was his to do with as he pleased.

His eyes narrowed, and she could feel his breathing

quicken. Without a word, he placed his arms beneath her and lifted her into his arms.

He carried her up the steps and took her into the bedroom they shared now. It was still broad daylight; Christine would be home from school soon.

He stopped in the middle of the room and let her slide down to her feet, and she couldn't prevent the whimper that escaped at the slide of her body over the iron-hard man flesh that distorted the shape of his trousers. Dropping his head, he kissed her, deeply and possessively, and she pressed herself against him and surrendered to his touch.

He ran a hand down over the curve of her hip. "This still seems like a dream. I imagined holding you so many times—"

She put a palm over his lips. "I'm real," she whispered. Too many feelings were ricocheting from thought to thought inside her head to continue talking. Tenderly, she reached up and replaced her palm with her lips, kissing him sweetly, outlining the shape of his lips with her tongue while his breathing grew heavy and his fingers began to knead her flesh.

He let her take the lead until his chest was heaving and his hard muscles were rigid with restraint, but finally, he took control of the kiss, thrusting his tongue into her in heady imitation of what his body told her he wanted. When she was writhing against him, he took her hands and set them at the buttons of his shirt, while he undressed her in turn.

She savored the first glimpse of curling hair at his throat when she slipped off his tie and opened the first buttons. Pulling his shirt wider, she stopped to press a kiss to the black curls matting his broad chest in the V neck of his T-shirt. She gripped the T-shirt in both hands and took it over his head, stroking her fingers over the wealth of black silk that extended under his arms and down his belly to disappear into the waistband of his pants.

"I wanted you to be fat and bald," she confessed as her nimble fingers undid his belt and the button on his pants.

He chuckled, though his eyes were intense and the muscles of his abdomen contracted involuntarily when the backs of her hands brushed against him. "I wanted you to be fat, period. And wrinkled." As he drew off her blouse and helped her step out of her skirt and half slip, he added, "But you looked as beautiful when I saw you at the funeral as you did the day I left. Like you had a private pipeline to the Fountain of Youth. It annoyed the hell out of me."

"It didn't show," she said wryly.

He grimaced. "I couldn't stop looking at your legs. It was an exercise in self-control not to reach out and touch."

She lowered her eyes flirtatiously. "I was grateful for all those hellish aerobics classes."

"So was I, believe me."

She laughed. But then he opened the clasp of her bra and slipped it from her shoulders, and the laughter died away at the raw wanting in his narrowed eyes. He shaped her breasts with his palms, his thumbs brushing her nipples until she clasped his wrists in protest. "Wait."

Placing her fingers on the zipper of his pants, she pulled steadily downward, conscious of the hard flesh pushing at the front of his briefs. Dax hissed in a breath, blew it out on a shaky sigh. She slipped her hands inside the waistband of his pants and slid them back and down until his buttocks were palmed in her hands and his trousers fell away. Beneath her palms, his skin was hot and silky, taut with sinew and muscle and arousal, and she felt the flesh flex in response to her touch.

He stepped out of his pants and removed the last of her clothing, then took her hands and held them wide. "I want to see you," he said hoarsely. "I want to touch you. I want to be inside you."

She shuddered, unbearably excited by his graphic words, by the unmistakable evidence of his desire as he stood naked before her.

He knelt before her. His hands grasped the backs of her thighs, then slid down to stroke her calves, her ankles, and every inch again on his way back up. "I must be a leg man," he said, his voice tight with strain, "because, honeybunch, these turn me on." He lifted one of her legs and bent it at the knee, hooking it over his shoulder.

The action spread her wide, made her vulnerable in a way only other women could understand, and she felt heat bloom in her cheeks. But then he opened the pouting secret flesh between her legs for his caresses, and she shuddered again, embarrassment and shyness forgotten. She gasped as he drew a single finger down her belly, tracing the soft flesh he'd discovered. He leaned forward and placed a kiss at the top of her thighs, against the curling blond hair he found there, and his hot breath blew over her. She quivered at the startling, intimate sensation. The leg she still stood on began to shake, and he gently replaced her other foot on the floor, then pulled her down to her knees facing him.

They were close, bodies brushing, and she could feel the throbbing strength of his arousal warm against her belly. Then he pulled her fully against him, seeking her mouth in a deep, questing kiss that had her clutching at his wide shoulders for balance.

"Please," she murmured when he let her breathe.

"Please what?" His voice was deep and husky. He lay her on the carpet and came down on her in a single fluid motion that showed her just how strong he really was. "Please...this?" He opened her legs and touched her with his fingers. She cried out incoherently, and he said, "Or please…this?'' And he parted her tender flesh and pushed himself slowly, steadily into her.

"Ah, that's good,'' he muttered when he was snug and deep within her. "Does that please you?''

She was too caught up in sensation to form a coherent answer. Her only response was a moan as her head began to thrash from side to side. He felt strong and solid where he pulsed inside her, huge and hungry. Her lips lifted as tense need tightened her muscles, and she moaned again when he began to move within her. Fast, faster, hard and harder he moved, slamming against her with a sweet violence that incited an equal reaction deep in her abdomen. She felt herself gathering as if for some great feat, his body pounding and pressing her, and with a thin cry she gave in to her body's demands, her back arching, heels digging into the rug, breath rushing in and out in a marathon of madness. Above her, his pace doubled, grew frantic as he surrendered himself to his body's urgings and thrust against her in rhythmic, rolling motions that slowly slipped to a halt as he spent himself inside her and gasped for breath denied.

"My God,'' he said, pressing a gentle kiss to her forehead. "How did I live without you?''

"I didn't live.'' Her heartbeat was slowing, but she lifted her legs and clasped them around his waist when he shifted. "I existed.''

Dax gave a long groan of satisfaction as her action carried him even deeper. "We're going to start living now.''

Long minutes later, Dax stirred, rousing her from a twilight state of dreaming.

"I wanted to be tender.'' His voice was a deep rumble beneath her ear.

They still lay on the rug, too content to move to the bed. "If I wanted tender, I'd have ordered a filet,'' she said. "But if you weren't happy with that effort, I suppose I can let you try it again.''

He chuckled. "Oh, I was happy with that effort. But I want you to be happy, too."

His words made her uncomfortable. She'd reentered this relationship with no expectations, and she didn't want to start expecting anything, not even his concern—that way, she couldn't be disappointed. To change the subject, Jillian raised her arm and looked at the watch she still wore. "School just ended. We have about fifteen minutes to make ourselves marginally presentable before we get company."

"Fifteen minutes?" Dax rolled so that she was beneath him again.

"More like ten, really. And I didn't have any lunch and I'm starving." On cue, her stomach gave a loud gurgling growl that made them both laugh.

As he rolled to his knees, stood and reached down to lift her to her feet, he said, "You're obviously not one of those people who can live on love alone."

"I guess not." The words only increased her uneasiness. It was the first time the word "love" had been mentioned between them. He'd obviously only meant it as a figure of speech, but it cut too close to the heart of her tender feelings for her to joke about it.

She began gathering up her discarded clothing, then moved to the door. "I'm going to get a quick shower. I unpacked inventory all day and it always makes me feel grimy. I'll be down in a few minutes."

After a shower as quick as she'd promised, she went down to the kitchen. Mrs. Bowley left at three-thirty on Fridays, and she was just putting on her light jacket as Jillian walked in.

"He's making omelets," the older woman said, winking at Jillian. "Don't let him wreck my kitchen."

"I never wreck kitchens," Dax said. "I've had to clean up after myself, so I've learned to avoid making messes in the first place."

There was an awkward moment of silence.

Then Mrs. Bowley picked up her knitting bag and her pocketbook. "Your mother would be glad to hear that," she informed him. "She was sure Jillian would whip you into shape when you got married. I guess it happened, anyway." She moved to the door, opening it and turning for a last warm smile. "I'll see you on Monday. Have a nice weekend. Oh, I almost forgot." She pointed to a piece of paper by the phone. "A man named Sullivan called. He wanted to know if you wanted to go to a ball game with him. You're supposed to call him back," she said to Jillian.

"Thank you." As the housekeeper closed the door on her way out, Jillian rose and reached for the handset. "Let me call him now before I forget."

"You're not going anywhere with him."

"Pardon?" She looked at Dax, surprised by the naked aggression in his tone.

"I said you are not—"

"I heard what you said." She knew her own voice was rising in volume but hurt and anger were rapidly taking over all else. "I just want to know *why* you said it."

"You're my wife." He set down his spatula and picked up a stack of plates with controlled motions. "I'm not one of those modern men who turns a blind eye to his wife's little liaisons."

"Little liaisons?" She spit out the words. "For your information, you *dolt,* Ronan's invitation would have been for both of us, and his wife would have been included in the party. It was probably a friendly gesture instigated by Deirdre."

There was sudden silence in the wake of her words. The air between them crackled with tension.

Finally, Dax blew out a breath. "Hell." He sounded more unsure of himself than she'd ever heard him sound in her life. "I guess I have to apologize, don't I?"

"I guess you do." Her voice was acid. She was still mad enough to airmail him to the moon. "I have never dated Ronan. I've only known him for a few years. In fact, Deirdre and I have been friends since we met at a business seminar six years ago. He and Deirdre met once while she was married to her first husband, and they met again after she was divorced. I think they got married two months later." She whirled around and stared out the window, tapping her toe in annoyance. "And why am I explaining myself to you?"

"I, ah, I'm sorry." The words were diffident, uttered slowly.

Surprised out of her pique, she turned around. She'd never seen Dax at a loss for words before, and his hangdog expression was so out of character that she found it hard to hang on to her anger. Softly, she asked, "Were you jealous?"

Dax set the plates on the table and came around to where she still stood. He stopped before her and reached out, sighing when she didn't pull away. Slipping his arms around her waist and pulling her against him, he said, "Let's just say I don't like to think of the other men who have been in your life."

"There haven't been many." It was important to her that he understand, and believe. "I've dated, but none of them were important."

"Good." He kissed her, and she responded to the desperation in his touch, knowing the same feeling. It killed something inside of her to think of him with other women. She had grown to adore Christine, but she still couldn't bring herself to think about how the child had come into Dax's life.

She had a feeling Dax's grand plan to ignore the past was fatally flawed.

* * *

Dinner had been nicer than he'd expected, Dax thought as they headed for their seats at Camden Yards the next night. He'd half expected hostility from Jillian's friends, but Ronan and Deirdre Sullivan were both friendly and relaxed with him.

He'd learned that they had two sons and a daughter, that the boys were Deirdre's sons from her previous marriage. Ronan's dark face lit up with warm emotion when he talked about his stepsons, and suddenly, Dax saw in his mind Jillian's smiling eyes showing him the perfect score Christine had received on her spelling test last week.

The realization that Jillian had opened her heart so completely to his daughter was humbling. He could only imagine how she must feel, being confronted with living, breathing proof of his infidelity every day, and when he put himself in her place…well, he just wasn't sure his heart was as big as hers. He took her hand more firmly in his as they walked along, reassuring himself with the warm clasp of her fingers and the quiet smile she slanted his way.

They walked through the throngs of people buying hats, T-shirts, pens, pins…every manner of memorabilia that could possibly be marketed to the public. Food stands flourished, offering hot dogs, pizza and popcorn. Clouds of cotton candy bounced above the heads of the crowd as a vendor carried his goods out to the rows of seats.

This was the first time he'd been to an Orioles game in the new ballpark, and the thing that impressed him the most was how clean it was. The old one had had an overall aura of grimy grimness. Your feet had stuck to the sticky floor with every step and you hated to enter the rest rooms because you never knew what you might find. But The Yard, as it was affectionately known…it was no wonder the team played to sellout crowds of enthusiastic fans every home game now.

Ronan led the way up the wide ramp and off at the first level.

And okay, he was impressed. The seats were just a few rows back along the first base line, affording them a great view of the pitching as well as the action in the field. He whistled softly. "You have to let me pay you for these," he said to Ronan over Jillian's head.

But Ronan shook his head. "Tax write-off. I use 'em to entertain people in the business." He grinned. "Didn't know you were an editor, did you?"

Dax laughed, too. He knew all about the way the IRS went after the self-employed.

The game was tense. The Mariners were breathing down their necks, trailing by a single run after the first few innings. He was surprised at how much Jillian knew about the team, but he shouldn't have been. She'd been the scorekeeper for Charles's high school team, he recalled.

The memory made him chuckle wryly to himself. No cheerleading for Jillian. She'd managed to be right on the bench near the boys.

Deirdre and Jillian excused themselves during the fifth inning to find a Ladies' room, and Ronan grinned across the empty seats at Dax. "Is this the life or what?"

"I'd be having more fun if they had a bigger lead."

Ronan laughed. "I know what you mean." He got up, juggling his popcorn and a giant soda, and plunked himself down in Jillian's seat next to Dax. "I see Jillian hasn't taken off any skin. You must be being a good boy."

Dax raised an eyebrow. "Maybe it's the other way around."

"That would be poetic justice." Ronan spoke absently, eyeing the field as the team manager walked to the mound to address his starting pitcher.

"Why?" This conversation was getting intensely interesting.

Ronan shrugged, his lips turning up in a half smile. "Let's just say Jill doesn't hesitate to wade in with her fists flying when she thinks one of her friends has been hurt."

Dax assessed Ronan instead of the ballfield. "I take it you've been the punching bag?"

"On one memorable occasion." The author grimaced. "Deirdre and I weren't…playing the game right for a while after we met. Jillian would have explained the rules to me but good if Frannie Ferris hadn't been there to referee."

Dax laughed. "That sounds like Jillian."

"But, on the other hand," Ronan said, "Once she's in your corner, she's there forever. I'm on the A-list now," he added complacently. Then he glanced at Dax, and his gold-flecked eyes sobered. "It was a hell of a shock to find out she got married right out of the blue."

Dax grimaced, honesty forcing him to admit, "It wasn't exactly out of the blue. We were engaged a long time ago. We had a pretty big misunderstanding and I left town. When I came back…" He shrugged. "There's never been anyone like her."

Ronan whistled. "*That* I can believe. Now I understand why she kept all those men at a distance." He grinned. "Though how she managed to keep them all as friends when she gave them their marching orders is something I wish I could figure out. It would be great in a book."

"She's always been able to wrap men around her little finger." He didn't want to think about the legions of men Jillian apparently had charmed while he was gone.

"Except for you." There was a clear question in R. A. Sullivan's voice.

"Except for me," he said flatly. He didn't particularly want to dissect his relationship with his wife in public.

"Deirdre's been worried," the other man said, his own voice cooling. "We've hardly heard from Jillian since she moved in with you."

"She's fine. Ask her."

"I will." Ronan got up from the seat and moved back to his own chair. "She's been alone for a long time. I'd really like to see her find someone who will treasure her the way I treasure my wife."

The women came back as he took his seat, and the prickly conversation ended. But it left Dax smarting from the tiny thorns in Ronan's words.

He treasured Jillian. More than Ronan would ever know.

Maybe it had taken him a while to realize it, but he didn't care about the past anymore. Charles was dead, and that chapter of their lives was gone forever.

He wanted to spend the rest of his life with her, find the happiness they should have begun to share seven years ago. He wanted things to be the way they were before he'd gone away, and Jillian seemed to want the same thing.

Nine

That night, they lay together in his bed after they'd made love.

Dax was stretched out on his back. His arm cuddled her close to his side and his fingers idly smoothed up and down over her upper arm.

"What are you thinking?" she asked.

She felt him shrug, and he turned his head to press his lips against her hair. "Just that I don't remember ever feeling this content with my life." He shifted slightly. "Do you feel it, too?"

She hesitated. "Yes," she said cautiously.

Beneath her hand, his ridged belly rose and fell in a silent laugh. "That was hardly a ringing endorsement."

She didn't laugh in return. She couldn't. And when she didn't speak, he rose on an elbow, looking down into her face in the dim light of the small lamp they'd left on.

"What's wrong?"

She drew in a breath. "I thought this would be enough, that I could make it be enough. But it's not."

"What, exactly, is it that isn't enough?"

"I can't just ignore the past." Raising a hand, she laid it against his cheek. "It really bothers me that you've never let me explain about the night you left."

"Oh, for Pete's sake!" He threw himself down on his back again. "I told you I don't care about that anymore. Isn't it enough that we're together again now?"

"No. It isn't. Not for me." Her voice was quiet and she swallowed. Maybe he didn't care anymore, but it was important to her that he listen to the truth. Somehow, though she couldn't quite fathom why, it insulted her that he was willing to take her even though he thought she had been unfaithful. It cheapened what they had, in her eyes.

There was silence in the bedroom, a heavy, hope-dulling silence.

"If it's that important to you, then I'll listen." There was no inflection of any kind in his voice.

She took a deep breath. "What you saw—what you thought that night—wasn't what you thought. You heard Charles tell me he loved me, but what you didn't hear was what led up to it. Charles was having an affair, but not with me."

"With who, then?"

"With the governor's wife."

"The *governor's wife!*" He sat up and looked down at her. "You expect me to believe that?"

"I expect you to listen," she said levelly. "The governor caught them together. Your mother was furious, because she was working to get some legislation through that would provide state tax relief for big corporations like Piersall, and she was afraid Charles might have killed her chances of gaining the governor's backing."

"I can see why, if it's true."

If it's true. He still was doubting every word that came out of her mouth.

She sat up, pulling the sheet around her and hugging her knees. Somehow, it didn't feel right to be naked in front of Dax right now. "Your mother went into full damage-control mode—she insisted Charles marry Alma Bender, a girl from Butler County whose family she knew. Charles had taken Alma out a few times, and apparently she was wild about him. Unfortunately, your idiot brother couldn't see what a gem she was."

"Until you pointed it out, of course." There was definite sarcasm in his voice, but she ignored it.

"Not exactly. Charles came whining to me the night he got caught, telling me the whole stupid story. Remember how we used to compare our dates?"

"I remember," he said. "You two told each other damn near everything."

"Not *everything.*" She made her voice teasing, trying to lighten the mood. "I never told him about us."

He didn't respond.

"Anyway, Charles came over that night after your mother issued her edict. I knew you were coming, and I didn't think he'd mind talking about it with you, either. He was lying on my bed like he always did—"

"With you in it."

"I was underneath the covers, he was on top of them. We were only hugging each other. And that's beside the point. You know we'd had late-night heart-to-heart talks for years. He expected me to sympathize with him, but instead I told him to grow up, to take responsibility for his own mess."

"And that's when I heard you tell him how much you loved him."

"Yes, you did." She refused to let him get under her

skin. "I *did* love your brother. Not the way I loved you, but he was my dearest friend."

Dax didn't say anything. She glanced at him; he wasn't looking at her, but at the far wall. His jaw was set although his face was perfectly composed.

"He told me he loved Alma like a friend, but that he could never marry her. He said he loved her the way he loved me. Dax, I swear to you that I never felt anything more than friendship for Charles. But in the end he did marry Alma, and then later, he began to think of her romantically. I know he loved her deeply until the moment they died."

She stopped. What else was there to say?

Dax hadn't moved. He still stared at the wall, but she knew he wasn't really seeing it. Seconds stretched into minutes, and her heart began to rupture again along the fault lines that so recently had been on the verge of repair.

He still didn't believe her. She'd been so sure that once she told him the truth, he'd believe. She must have been crazy.

She sighed in defeat, and the sound hitched at the end. Furious with herself, she lay back down. She'd wait until he turned out the light and then she'd leave the room. In the meantime, she *would not* cry.

Behind her, she felt Dax also lie back down. Then the hard length of him pressed against her back and curled around her, spoon-fashion, and his arm came over her. The pain that accompanied his embrace was so exquisite she wondered if a person had ever actually died from a broken heart.

"Honey-bunch."

"What?" She held herself rigid.

"Do you feel better now?"

"Do I—?" She rolled over to face him. *"What?"*

"You've wanted to tell me this for a long time. Do you

feel better now?'' He smoothed a hand down her hip. ''Now we can consider the slate clean, and we can start again.''

''You don't believe me.''

He was silent for a moment. Then he sighed. ''I don't know. I honestly don't know. But I don't care, either. It happened a long time ago. All I want is for us to forget the past and enjoy what we have now.'' He pulled her onto her back. ''I care about you, more than I've ever cared for any other woman. Can't that be enough?''

It might be as close to a declaration of love as she would ever get from him again. Pride and integrity warred with emotion. She wanted him to believe her, to believe *in* her, more than she'd ever wanted anything in her whole life. He couldn't—wouldn't—give her that.

If she wanted him, she'd have to set aside her dream of settling their misunderstanding. Could she live with less than all of him her entire life?

Then he put a hand to her cheek, and his thumb rubbed along her lower lip. ''Please don't leave me,'' he said in a husky voice. ''I need you.''

And she was lost. If she refused him, she'd spend the rest of her life as lonely as she'd been until he came home again. Her heart might never be whole, her self-worth might have a hole the size of Butler County in it, but Dax needed her. He'd admitted it, he'd asked her to stay.

She loved him too much to do otherwise.

Fall finally was beginning to make its presence known, and there was a nip in the air as Jillian walked into the bar where she'd agreed to meet Roger on Wednesday afternoon, hanging her lightweight autumn coat near the door before surveying the crowd. Roger was waiting for her in a booth against the wall, and as she slid into the seat opposite him, he rose and gave her a very correct kiss on the cheek.

"Hello," she said. "How have you been, Roger?"

"Not so great, if you want to know the truth."

Her euphoric mood began to dissipate. She hated to see her friends unhappy. "Uh-oh. What's the matter?"

"Your husband is what's the matter," Roger said quietly.

"Dax?" She was bewildered. She'd been so pleased that Roger hadn't lost his job that she'd never imagined he might be unhappy with Dax. "What do you mean?"

"Have you looked at the financial records for the company?" he asked her. "Oh, I know you wouldn't understand what you were looking at, but it's very clear to anyone who can decipher it."

"What's very clear?" She realized Roger had no idea of the extent of her involvement in Dax's decision-making. For the moment, it seemed best to keep it that way.

Roger sighed heavily. "Oh, Jillian, I hate to burden you with this. If I weren't so concerned for Piersall, I'd just forget it."

She was going to strangle him if he didn't start talking. But she waved an airy hand. "Oh, Roger, you know nothing bothers me for long. Why don't you tell me all about this problem you think you have?"

"Well…" Roger appeared to weigh his words. Finally he nodded. "As a stockholder, you have a right to know." He took a deep breath. "I think your husband is trying to ruin the company."

"Ruin the company!" It wasn't hard to make her face appear suitably shocked. "How could he do that?"

"When someone has voting control of the board, as Dax does at the moment, it's very easy for that someone to make unilateral decisions that aren't necessarily in *everyone's* best interests, if you see what I mean."

"I don't think I do."

"Your husband has been systematically undermining all the good business practices we've instituted at Piersall over the years. The company soon won't be able to sustain such a drain on its resources, and as that begins to show in our financial reports, stock prices are going to go down. I think he's making a deliberate effort to make the company look weak so that he can acquire more of the stock at rock-bottom prices."

She didn't have to fake looking aghast. So *he* was the one! Roger was accusing Dax of the very thing he'd been maneuvering for even before Charles died. A red mist of rage rose as she realized this man had fully intended to betray dear, gentle Charles, who had trusted him implicitly, and now was doing his best to ruin *her* family, Dax's unceasing efforts, Christine's birthright. Aloud, she said, "But I don't understand. If the company's going bad, then the stock is worthless, right?"

Roger gave her an indulgent smile. "Yes, but you see, it works like this. If the stock isn't worth much, someone— Dax—could buy a lot at a low price. Then he steps in and hires new people, puts the firm back on good footing, and sells the stock at a much higher price. Owning so much of it would mean he could sell off enough to make a significant sum and still retain enough to control the board."

"You don't mean…he'd line his pockets at our expense?"

Roger nodded. Very glumly. "I'm afraid that's exactly what I mean. But you don't have to worry. This shouldn't affect you at all, if you just go along with him."

"And pretend there's nothing wrong?" She pitched her voice high and tremulous, and Roger reached over the table and patted her hand.

"I'm so sorry to be the one to have to tell you this."

"But—but isn't there something you can do about it?

That is why you told me, right? Because we still have a chance to stop him?" It really was too bad, she thought, that she hadn't thought to bring a pocket tape recorder. But who would have suspected?

Roger leaned forward. "There's only one way, dear girl. At the next board meeting, you would have to vote against him." He paused. "I realize that's asking a lot of you—"

"Roger, Jillian. Good afternoon. May I join you?" Gerard Kelvey stood beside their table.

Roger stood immediately and made appropriate noises of surprise, but his relief was so obvious that even if it hadn't seemed like a too-convenient chance meeting, she'd have known immediately. Gerard, who'd been a stockholder since before she was born, a friend to Dax's father Travers before him—Gerard Kelvey was working with Roger to run Dax out of his own family business.

As Gerard seated himself across from her, Roger looked him in the eye. "I'm glad you stopped by. I have been sharing our concerns about the direction Dax is taking the company with Jillian."

"And?"

Even as a child, she'd never liked Kelvey, she recalled. He was one of those adults who simply gave you the creeps. Now she knew why. He looked just like a weasel. A beady-eyed, slimy little creature who wouldn't hesitate to climb into the nest and steal the golden egg.

"I'm shocked," she pronounced. "Simply shocked."

"So was I," Gerard pronounced in mournful tones.

"As was I." Roger just couldn't resist pouring it on.

"However," she said, giving each man a devastating smile, "I doubt we are shocked for the same reason."

Identical looks of noncomprehension followed her statement. She went on.

"I have an accounting degree. Dax has been sharing the

books and all the interesting things he's found in them with me for weeks.''

Roger's eyes bulged wide. Gerard's wrinkled face sagged in utter shock as each of the men absorbed the unexpected information.

"Which one of you is Shallott, Limited? Or whichever silly little corporate name you've picked this week?" she demanded. "Or didn't you think Dax was smart enough to catch that? He's known all along that someone was snapping up stock, but neither of us was too worried about it because *our family* controls more than half." She stood. "I would hate to waste your time, gentlemen, so let me be brief. My family will continue to administer Piersall Industries in the competent hands of my husband. My votes are his, and his votes are mine."

Gerard looked at Roger in disgust. "You told me you'd be able to manage her. This has all been a monumental waste of time." Without another word, the older man stood and plowed through the crowd to the door.

There was utter silence in the wake of his departure. The sounds of other patrons didn't even register with her. Jillian looked across the table at Roger's white face. "Gerard's right," she said in a tight voice, battling with everything in her to control the rage she felt. "This has all been a monumental waste of time. I would never betray Dax. He's the only man I've ever loved."

As exit lines went, it was a grand one. Too bad she was too angry to fully appreciate it. It took her fully half the hour-long drive home to quit seething, and the other half to make a determined effort to be cheerful.

Dax had been right to be concerned. But there was no need. When she could discuss it rationally, maybe in a month or four, she'd tell him about the meeting and they'd laugh over it together.

Then again, she thought with the touch of fatalism that

was becoming her constant companion these days, Dax didn't believe her when she tried to explain about Charles; why should he believe something like this? It would all fade away eventually, anyhow, when no further movement of the stock occurred, and Dax would forget he'd ever worried about it.

His week seemed to last forever.

On Friday, Dax walked up the stairs to the bedroom he shared with Jillian. He wasn't in a good mood. Three of the larger stockholders had sold within the past week.

One apologetically called him after the transaction and told him he just couldn't pass on the kind of offer that had been made. He'd begun making calls and discovered the other two sales. Naomi Stell had informed him that someone had made her a very generous offer as well. She'd declined, she assured him and no, she didn't know who because it came through her broker and it was confidential.

If the Shallot firm, or whoever the hell they really were, had been the purchasers in the most recent day of trading, they could possibly control as much as thirty-four percent of the votes right now.

Technically, he supposed he shouldn't be worrying. Between the shares he and Jillian held and Christine's which he controlled until she reached her majority, they controlled the direction of the board.

As long as they voted together.

The fact that Jillian had never turned over voting control of her stock to him hadn't gone unnoticed. He'd never pursued it because he didn't want to make an issue of something that probably was nothing. She was his wife, and they shared a concern for the company.

And there was no way he was going to risk upsetting her, given the funny, unusually quiet way she'd been acting ever since last Sunday night when she'd forced him to listen to her story about what went on between Charles and her that night.

What did she expect from him? Why wasn't it enough that he was willing to forgive her?

He wanted to believe her. He really did. But he just wasn't sure...,

What he wanted was to forget those seven years had ever happened.

"Daddy?" Christine came out of her room. She was wearing the ballet costume Jillian had given her for her birthday and she carried a doll, also wearing a ballet outfit with pink satin shoes.

"Hi, honey. Are you getting ready to go onstage and dance for all your fans?"

She giggled. The sound was music to his ears; he realized that she was beginning to act much more like a little girl and less like the inhibited, miniature adult he'd come to expect.

"Daddy, Aunt Marina called Jillian a little while ago. She wants to know if I can come and *stay overnight* tonight!" Christine sounded as awed as if she'd been invited to meet her favorite movie star. "Can I? Tomorrow's Saturday and she said I can stay all day."

He pretended to consider the request. "Well, I suppose you can do that. If you promise not to eat with your fingers or burp at the table."

She giggled again. "You're silly, Daddy." He could tell from her beaming face that she knew his answer was a yes, and he watched as she bounced down the stairs, ponytail—courtesy of Jillian this morning—bobbing. "I'm gonna go play in the yard with Elizabeth."

He very nearly asked who Elizabeth was before he realized she was speaking of the doll. And as he went to find his wife, he decided that marrying her was the smartest thing he'd ever done if Jillian had the ability to make his daughter that happy.

He caught her unaware as she was folding her clothing into the drawers in their bedroom. He stood in the doorway for a few moments before she saw him, simply drinking in the sight of her in his home.

Then she turned slightly and he could see her face in the mirror, though she hadn't seen him yet.

And he felt a chill dribble icy droplets down his spine. She looked sad. More than sad. Sorrowful. Sorrow-filled. They'd laughed about not getting enough sleep but this was something far different. Something he'd seen on her face a number of times recently when she thought she was alone.

An ugly thought sneaked into his head. Was she still mourning Charles? A clear memory rose to the surface of his mind, of Jillian sitting on his lap in the study downstairs. He'd mentioned Charles's name and her entire body had tensed. Tightened. He'd forced himself to ignore it at the time, but it hadn't been forgotten.

Then she raised her gaze and saw him in the mirror. Her face fell into its customary smiling lines and her eyes lit with the special warmth she saved only for him. "Hey there, handsome!"

He crossed the rug to her, kissing her lightly and taking the stack of clothing from her so that he could fit his already hardening body into its familiar niche against her. "Mm-m-m. I've waited for this all day."

"The door's open and Chrissy's home," she warned with a smile. "So you're going to have to wait a little longer."

He didn't smile in return. "Honey-bunch, are you happy?"

She stilled in his arms. "Don't I seem happy?"

"I think so," he said, running his palms absently up and

down her back, aware that she hadn't answered him. "Are you?"

She moved closer, nuzzling into his neck, pressing small kisses up and down his throat, and he couldn't see her eyes. "I'm happy," she said, her words muffled against his neck. "Every day I wake up and pinch myself to be sure this is real."

"Well, get used to it," he said, his disquieting thoughts fading under the passion her slender figure aroused in him. "It's going to be real for the rest of your life."

"I'll take it a day at a time," she said.

The statement bothered him and he realized that she had avoided any discussion of their future so far. But she was on tiptoe against him, taking his earlobe gently between her teeth, and his body told him to quit worrying. His life was almost perfect. Why look for trouble?

He tore himself away from her and shut the bedroom door, locking it decisively. "The door's closed," he said unnecessarily. "How about I convince you that I'm real?"

Her beautiful face dissolved into lines of humor, underlaid with a slumberous passion that turned her blue eyes mysterious and inviting. "I'm hard to convince. This might take awhile."

Two hours later, she drove Christine over to Marina's for the night. By the time they left, Christine was so excited he thought he might have to peel her off the ceiling. As the door closed behind them, he headed for the study. Might as well try to make sense of these puzzling numbers one more time until Jillian got home and they'd have the house to themselves. He could already see them relaxing in the Jacuzzi tub with cold drinks.

Twenty minutes later, the doorbell interrupted his train of thought.

He rose and walked into the foyer, pulling open the

heavy door. To his surprise, Gerard Kelvey stood on the other side.

"Gerard. Come in. What can I do for you?" Automatically, he offered the older man a hand. Kelvey had been one of his father's cronies, and Dax had never particularly liked him. He suspected the feeling was mutual. He knew the man didn't approve of his business decisions. He'd voted against Dax's proposals consistently every time something came up.

Gerard hesitated, a mannerism out of character. "I, ah, I need to talk with you, Dax. It's about the business."

"Would you like to come into the study?" Dax ushered the older stockholder into the study and got him a drink. Then he leaned back against the edge of his desk. "Now, what's on your mind?"

Kelvey cleared his throat. "You're, ah, aware that there's been significant stock movement over the past month, I'm told."

Told by whom? Aloud, he said, "That's correct. Are you one of those who's been buying?"

Kelvey nodded. "I was."

Dax noticed his use of the past tense. "I wondered why," he said. "After all, it isn't as though you could amass enough to influence the direction of the vote, given the quantity I hold. Who else is involved?"

"Roger. This was his idea." Gerard shook his head, apparently disgusted with himself. "I never should have listened to him. Your father...your father was my friend. He offered me an opportunity to invest in Piersall thirty years ago and I've betrayed that trust." He looked at Dax. "I apologize. If you want to buy me out, I'll understand."

So Roger Wingerd had been the one cheating Charles. It would have been easy enough, given the amount of trust Charles had placed in the man. He rose and held out his hand to Kelvey. "Thank you for coming forward. No harm has been done. As I said, Wingerd can't purchase enough stock to affect my policies.''

"He could if Jillian was willing to vote with him.''

Dax froze. *If Jillian was willing to vote with him.* Hadn't that been his concern all along?

Just for an instant, he allowed himself to wonder if she would do that. The night in the study when he'd mentioned Charles's name while telling her about the stock shifts flashed through his mind. She'd gone rigid for a moment, then he'd seen her gradually make herself relax. He'd assumed her reaction was to his mention of Charles's name. But maybe it was more than that.

No. Jillian wouldn't do anything like that. She told you her shares were yours, that you'd vote together.

She'd also told him she hadn't slept with his brother. And had stayed with him even when he hadn't been able to tell her unconditionally that he believed her. Was that the way a guilty woman would have acted?

Jillian loves you. She's never knowingly betrayed you in her life.

The enormity of his error struck him like a grenade exploding squarely in the dirt at his feet, blowing to bits all his carefully nursed anger, all his suspicions and resentments. She'd told him the truth all along—about everything—and he'd refused to believe her.

What had he done?

A tread on the stairs had his head jerking up, had him leaping to the door of the study. Jillian was halfway up the main staircase. When she heard him coming, she turned, and he stopped in his tracks, shocked by the sight of her white face.

"Honey-bunch...'' He held out his hand.

"You thought it might be me.'' Her lips trembled and she pressed a fist against her mouth a moment. "I saw the look on your face when Gerard mentioned my name. You thought I might be part of it.''

"No, I—only for a minute." He started toward the foot of the stairs but stopped as she immediately turned and fled. *"Damn it!"*

He practically booted Kelvey out the door, barely giving the man a chance to stammer out a full explanation of the meeting Roger had arranged with Jillian before he turned and sprinted for the stairs. He knew what she had to be thinking.

And it was true.

Ten

She slammed and locked the door of her room. No, not her room. Simply the one where she'd slept when she first came into this house. For a moment, she leaned against the cool wood, pressing a hand to her pounding heart and gasping in deep, harsh breaths of air that made her chest hurt.

When she'd come home, she'd seen the strange car in the driveway. She'd paused in the door of the study, seeing Gerard, hearing his damning words—

He could if Jillian was willing to vote with him.

And she'd seen the doubt in her husband's eyes.

"Jillian?" The doorknob rattled and she leaped away from it as if it was suddenly electrified. "Honey, let me come in. We have to talk."

She didn't answer. She couldn't.

"Please, honey, don't shut me out. Let me explain."

Let me explain.

What could he possibly have to explain? She felt like

she'd been trying her whole life to explain herself to Dax. And ultimately, it had done no good. Not one little bit. If anything, he mistrusted her now even more than he had the first day he'd returned. She was never going to be able to make him believe in her again—it was time to quit fooling herself.

"All right." He was still there, just on the other side of that door, and she didn't think she could bear to be so close to him. "I could get the key and unlock this, but I'll respect your privacy. We'll talk in the morning."

Slowly, she walked across the room to the big bed. Crawling up onto the cover, she pulled a pillow to her and clutched it against her chest, cushioning the ache inside as she forced herself to take deep, calming breaths.

First thing in the morning, she would leave. She needed to start hunting another location for Kids' Place, and she had to warn her neighbors what to expect. Since she would be breaking the prenuptial agreement, she doubted she could expect any mercy from Dax.

But she couldn't stay here any longer. Not another day. She'd been wrong to think she could make this marriage work and even stupider to allow herself to hope that they could resolve the past.

And she'd been wrong to think she could live without his love for the rest of their lives.

Dawn came, and with it, came wakefulness. Dax climbed from the depths of slumber and instantly realized Jillian wasn't in his arms. He was alone in his bed. An instant of fear gripped him, until the clock showed him it was barely six in the morning.

He sincerely doubted she'd gone anywhere yet. He stretched and rose. There was no need to dress since he'd slept in his clothes in case Jillian attempted a midnight sneak-away.

In the bathroom, he remembered Chris was still at Ben's. And since it was Saturday, Mrs. Bowley wasn't around. It would be just Jillian and him.

Perfect.

He'd always known she was extraordinary. All these years, he'd compared other women to her without even knowing it—and there'd been no contest. No one else had even made the first cut.

He'd lain awake for hours last night, reliving every stupid, insensitive thing he'd ever said to her. He wouldn't blame her if she didn't love him anymore.

A ball of ice lodged in his gut at that thought. Once before, when he'd thought of how she'd accepted Christine, it had occurred to him that her heart was bigger than his. Now he was going to pray that he'd been right, that she could forgive him.

He took a deep breath. He just didn't know—he'd hurt her over and over. No matter what it took, how he had to accomplish it, he had to shatter the wall she'd built around her. He wanted Jillian. Tears, sorrows, joys and all.

But even if he couldn't have her, it was his turn to heal. If she didn't want him back, didn't want to try to save something of what they'd once had, she still deserved to be the vivid, shimmering butterfly with whom he'd first fallen in love.

Crossing the hall, he was smiling, his plan of action determined. Kid gloves wouldn't work; he knew that from last night's patient approach. Jillian might not know it, but she was coming back to life.

Her door wasn't locked now. He found her exactly where he'd anticipated—packing—when he swung open it open without knocking, and he leaned against the door frame. Her head jerked up in alarm, but she said nothing, only turned back to her packing when she saw him.

There was little life in her again this morning. Of all the

things that had happened since he'd come home, this one bothered him most. Slowly, but surely, the woman he knew was disappearing.

Her shoulders slumped as she moved from dresser to bed and back again, and her movements were sparse and sluggish, as if the effort were almost too much. Apparently, it was, because after another moment she let her hands fall from her task and picked up a single black overnight bag.

"I'll send someone over tomorrow to get the rest of it." She made a languid gesture in the direction of the closet and attempted a smile. But he was blocking the door, not bothering to smile, and after one wary glance at him, she remained standing in the center of the room.

"Running away?" His words were deliberately provocative. Where was the woman who'd stood toe-to-toe with him and spit in his eye? Suddenly, he was furious with himself. How could he have crushed her spirit this way?

"No. Just leaving." It was as hollow as the look in her eyes.

"Like I said, running away." His teeth gritted together with the effort to keep from throwing the damned suitcase out the window.

"Unlike you, *I* do not run away from anything," she said, spacing each word carefully.

He raised an eyebrow, hating to hurt her more, but determined to reach beyond the despair to the still-vital core he knew, he *prayed*, was there. "Sure looks like running to me."

"Maybe you're right." She dropped the bag and faced him. "After all, you are the resident expert on the fine art of leaving your loved ones." Her brows drew together so fiercely that they could have been a single line. Her cheeks were growing pink, and he thought he saw the first sparks of anger flaring in her eyes. Good.

Delighted, at last, to have found a button to push, he

gave her the nastiest smile he could muster. "That's a good excuse, isn't it? You've blamed me for just about everything that went wrong with your life since I left."

"That is *not* true." It was a hiss.

"Oh, yes, it is." He took a step toward her; she stood her ground. "You never married, never had a child of your own. It bothered the hell out of you when you found out about Christine. And having to share your husband with his child by another woman is another strike against me."

"All right, I admit it. I was prepared to loathe the kid. But I didn't. I *can't*." Her voice grew in volume until she was shouting. "She's not just the combined genes of you and this woman you like to throw in my face. She's a person in her own right and I love that person."

She pointed an accusing finger at him. "You want to know what really sticks in my throat? I'll tell you! It doesn't have a damn thing to do with Christine." Her eyes blazed with fury. "I thought we loved each other, Dax. *We were going to get married* because we loved each other. And the first chance you got, you were hopping in the sack with someone else. It tells me exactly how much I really meant to you all those years ago."

"I told you why." He'd wanted to bring her to life again, but he hadn't bargained on the naked aggression radiating from her. Tears, collapsing in his arms, maybe, but not an eruption the size of Vesuvius. "And you're wrong. You meant everything to me."

"I don't care," she spat at him. "Leaving me was one thing. But you barely got out of town before you found somebody to replace me."

It would have been a good time to remind her that no woman could ever replace her. He'd been afraid his Jillian had vanished forever, crushed beneath the sorrows her life had piled on her shoulders...with his help. The blazing fire in her eyes was almost a welcome relief.

"I hung around like a pathetic little puppy, waiting for your forgiveness for something I never even did," she said bitterly. "And last night, I learned just what you really think of me. It was educational, Dax. It really was."

"I knew you would never vote against me," he said defensively. "And I was right. Gerard told me all about your meeting with Roger." His voice dropped. "He told me I was damned lucky to have a woman who loved me like you do."

"I don't love you anymore," she said, and again her voice began to rise. "I wouldn't love you if you were the last man left on earth."

"Liar." He hoped. He started toward her, intending to calm her down.

Then she picked up the china clock on the nightstand.

"Hey, wait a min—" He just had time to duck as the clock smashed into a million flying pieces of crockery and broken metal innards above his head. "Honey-bunch, I—"

"Don't you dare call me that stupid name!" A book thudded against the wall to his left; he feinted and when she hurled a relatively harmless pillow his way, he moved in before she could get her hands on anything else lethal.

She saw him coming, and turned to dash around the bed, but he caught her with a flying tackle that sent them bouncing and rolling over the mattress and crashing to the floor. He twisted, rolling so that she didn't take the brunt of the fall, then had to move fast not to lose his grip.

"It's not a stupid name," he panted. How the hell could somebody who looked so fragile give him such a hard time? He grabbed her wrists before she could scratch him, and shifted his weight just in time to avoid the knee she tried to ram into parts of him that definitely didn't like knees.

"It is," she said.

"Honey-bunch. Honey-bunch, honey-bunch, honey-bunch.'' Finally, he had her on her back, subduing her with his superior weight pressing her into the rug. Noticing, as he did so, how damn good she felt beneath him. Thank God *that* had never changed.

"Stop it, Dax.'' She was still glaring at him, and if those looks were bullets, he wouldn't be breathing. "Go practice your charms on somebody else. I want to leave.''

"We had a deal,'' he reminded her.

"Null and void. I'll sign my stock over to you.''

"Will you? Too bad,'' he said. "Because I'm still not letting you go. Is there anything else you want to get off your chest?''

"Other than you? Oh, you bet there is. It isn't enough that you came back, you ground me into teeny tiny pieces, and you presented me with your daughter. No, you have to end every argument we have like *this*.'' She thrust her hips upward, into him, in an angry challenge. "If you didn't outweigh me and you couldn't seduce me every time you touched me, I'd have brushed you off long ago.''

He laughed. "Isn't that the point?'' He dropped his head until he was inches from her face. "You've been leading men around by the nose for so many years you're just a poor sport when it doesn't work. Besides, that seduction thing works two ways. Before you get off on another raving tack, maybe you should think about the reason we keep coming back to each other.''

"Sex.'' The word was flat and sullen.

"It's more than that.'' He shook his head, then his voice gentled. "It's far more than that. You're the other half of my soul. And I'm yours. Apart, we only exist. You said that once.''

"At this point, *existing* would be a treat. It beats having my heart ripped out.''

The pain in her voice sobered him immediately. "Forgive me.''

"For what? For being born?"

"For being the untrusting jerk who walked away from the only woman in the world he'll ever love. I realized last night—when you rushed out without letting me explain—that I do trust you. I believe you never shared more than friendship with Charles. The only person to blame for the years we lost is my own stupid self." He dropped his head and gently kissed her forehead, praying that he was getting through. "I still love you, Jillian. You're the only woman who's ever owned my heart."

Her eyes filled with tears. Beneath him, her body went limp and he felt her chest heave as she tried to suppress sobs. "Do you know how badly I wanted to hear that? How many years I dreamed that you'd tell me you love me again? You—you *creep*."

The first faint stirrings of relief began to rise within him. He took a deep breath, forcing himself to stay calm. "Say you won't leave."

"Tell me one good reason we should stay together."

He hesitated, took a deep breath. "I don't want to live without you. If you send me away, if you leave, you'll be making a mistake as monstrous as the one I made all those years ago." He let go of her wrists and brought one hand down to stroke her cheek.

Eyes the color of a summer sky, as wet as an April morning, searched his, seeing deep into his soul. "I'd like to believe we could—"

"Then let yourself believe, and we can."

She brought her hands to his shoulders, caressed his back. "I don't want to live without you, either. But—"

"Let me say it again," he said. "I was wrong. We can't forget the past. But we can accept it, and overcome it." He risked a smile. "And I know you've always risen to a challenge."

"You know me better than *I* know me. I surrender." She

brought her hands to the back of his head and tugged his mouth to hers, pressing a sweet kiss to his lips.

It took a fraction of a second for him to realize he'd won. His future was bright again, as bright as the hair of the woman he held in his arms. As comprehension came, desire rose, and he deepened the kiss, stroking his tongue around hers repeatedly until she tore her mouth away for a gasp of breath.

"I love you, Dax."

He shifted his body more surely over hers, and the future stretched before him, full of promise and possibilities, and above all, the woman he loved. "I love you, too, honeybunch. You'll never know how much."

Her eyes gleamed, and she wriggled beneath him. "Gee, I guess you'll have to keep showing me."

A long time later, she raised her head from where it rested on his chest. "I'm starting to like this floor sex."

He laughed. "Good. There are lots of floors in this house. Why limit ourselves?"

"Of course, when I'm pregnant, we may have to forgo the floors for a while."

He didn't answer her for a moment and when she looked up at him, she caught the diamond glitter of tears brightening his eyes.

When he finally was able to speak, his voice was husky and deep with emotion. "When you're pregnant, we won't take a single, solitary chance. I want you to have my child more than anything I've ever wanted in my life. Except your love."

My love. As she wrapped her arms around him, feeling her body soften in welcome, she knew it was real. Dax had truly come home.

Epilogue

It was an Indian summer in September again. What a difference a year made, Jillian thought as she watched Dax leap out of his lawn chair, cheering. He was simply irresistible.

They all were, she thought fondly, looking at the four men whooping and trading high-fives when the radio announced that their beloved Orioles' center-fielder just smacked a grand slam over the padded center field fence to win the game by one run in the bottom of the ninth.

Dax, Ronan, and Ben slapped shoulders and pounded backs, while Jack pounded his chest and howled in a hilariously off-target attempt to mimic Tarzan. No wonder Frannie called him that occasionally.

Well, Jack might be a big clown, but when it came to loving Frannie he was more than serious. He was so dedicated it still brought a lump to her throat just watching them together with Alexa, Ian and little Brittany.

Christine had Brittany right now, playing peekaboo and making the toddler laugh while Frannie fixed herself a sandwich at the picnic table in Jillian's yard. Chrissy was going to miss all these little kids when school started next week, she thought, smiling as her stepdaughter intercepted a hug from a too-enthusiastic Maureen. The littlest Sullivan was two and a half now, and she chattered nonstop as she headed for the table where Deirdre sat talking with Frannie and Marina.

Ronan grabbed Maureen just as she was about to climb into her mother's plate, and she shrieked in protest. But her crying turned immediately to giggles when he set her on his shoulders.

Dear Ronan. He'd healed Deirdre's wounded heart and wrapped her in such love and tenderness that Jillian had forgiven him for behaving like a randy teenager during his courtship of Dee. And who was *she* to throw stones, she thought ruefully, recalling the early months of her reunion with Dax. They hadn't been able to speak two civil words in succession, but their bodies had known *exactly* what to say.

So she couldn't blame Ronan. Besides, he was a really good guy. He had taken his stepsons into his heart and his life in a manner that still awed her. And anyone, she thought in amusement, watching as Ronan corralled Tommy and Lee—who had just finished shaking a Pepsi can and were about to open it directly behind Jack's back—*anyone* who took on those two deserved a gold star in his crown on Judgment Day.

Ben warned Jack of the impending danger and the big man turned and began stalking the boys, who screeched as they beat a hasty retreat. Ben was laughing, too, until he realized that John Benjamin had picked up the abandoned can, tugging at the tab with all his miniature might. Then he moved with the speed and grace she'd always admired, snagging his thirteen-month-old son and whirling him in circles to distract him until Marina came running, protesting that John B. would throw up if he didn't stop.

Marina had been incredibly lucky to have found a man like Ben so soon after being widowed. Jillian had thought he was annoyingly autocratic at first, and she still thought it, sometimes, but the similarities between him and her tall, dark, *autocratic* husband were amazing. They'd even been born in the same year.

As the adults began to round up the children for ice cream, Dax left the crowd and came over to the chair where she sat, half-turned away from the others.

"How's he doing?" he asked, bending to survey his two-month-old son, nursing at Jillian's breast. Then he bent and pressed a lingering kiss to her forehead. "And how are you doing? Getting tired? I'll play host if you want to go and lie down for a nap."

Jillian shook her head, smiling up at him as she pressed a gentle finger against her nipple, releasing the suction Charlie created as he suckled. Her heart swelled with love as she looked from her husband to their infant son.

She held Charlie up and Dax took the tiny body, putting him to his shoulder as he rubbed the little back and crooned deep, gentle noises.

"He's fine," she said as she rearranged her clothing. "And so am I—fine and ready to party."

"When are you not?" Dax grinned as he offered her his free hand, pulling her out of the chair and wrapping his arm securely around her. And as they walked to rejoin their family and their friends, she realized it was true. She *was* fine.

Her life had come full circle. And though she would always regret the lost years, she had moved on. After years of looking backward and covering her past with layers of dust, she was polishing her love to a high shine.

*   *   *   *   *

If you enjoyed what you just read, then we've got an offer you can't resist!

Take 2 bestselling love stories FREE!

Plus get a FREE surprise gift!

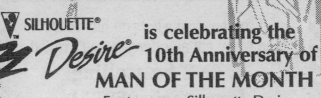

SILHOUETTE®

Desire® is celebrating the 10th Anniversary of
MAN OF THE MONTH

For ten years Silhouette Desire
has been giving readers the ultimate in
sexy, irresistible heroes.

**So come celebrate with your
absolute favorite authors!**

MAN
of the
Month

JANUARY 1999
BELOVED by Diana Palmer—
SD #1189 Long, Tall Texans

FEBRUARY 1999
**A KNIGHT IN RUSTY ARMOR
by Dixie Browning—**
SD #1195 The Lawless Heirs

MARCH 1999
**THE BEST HUSBAND IN TEXAS
by Lass Small—**
SD #1201

APRIL 1999
BLAYLOCK'S BRIDE by Cait London—
SD #1207 The Blaylocks

MAY 1999
LOVE ME TRUE by Ann Major—
SD #1213

Available at your favorite retail outlet, only from

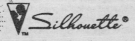

Silhouette®

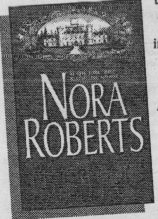
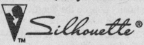

COMING NEXT MONTH